NOW HE HAD TIME TO BE AFRAID

The herd was bought, and now it was surging toward the railroad, with French Williams' outfit driving it.

But French dealt harshly with a dude. If Chantry stayed with the cattle drive, he'd be rich on the proceeds. If he dropped out—and French would try to make sure of that—Chantry would be ruined. And probably dead.

Sooner or later, Chantry knew, he would have to shoot it out.

NORTH TO THE RAILS
Louis L'Amour's action-packed novel
of a civilized man's courage in a savage
and lawless land.

Bantam Books by Louis L'Amour

Ask your bookseller for the books you have missed

BORDEN CHANTRY
BRIONNE
THE BROKEN GUN
THE BURNING HILLS
THE CALIFORNIOS
CALLAGHEN
CATLOW
CHANCY
CONAGHER
DARK CANYON
DOWN THE LONG HILLS
THE EMPTY LAND
FALLON
THE FERGUSON RIFLE
THE FIRST FAST DRAW
FLINT
GUNS OF THE TIMBER-
 LANDS
HANGING WOMAN
 CREEK
THE HIGH GRADERS
HIGH LONESOME
HOW THE WEST WAS
 WON
THE IRON MARSHAL
THE KEY-LOCK MAN
KID RODELO
KILLOE
KILRONE
KIOWA TRAIL
THE MAN CALLED
 NOON
THE MAN FROM
 SKIBBEREEN
MATAGORDA
THE MOUNTAIN
 VALLEY WAR
NORTH TO THE RAILS
OVER ON THE DRY SIDE
THE PROVING TRAIL

THE QUICK AND THE
 DEAD
RADIGAN
REILLY'S LUCK
THE RIDER OF LOST
 CREEK
RIVERS WEST
SHALAKO
SITKA
TAGGART
TUCKER
UNDER THE SWEET-
 WATER RIM
WAR PARTY
WESTWARD THE TIDE
WHERE THE LONG
 GRASS BLOWS

Sackett Titles by
Louis L'Amour

---

1. SACKETT'S LAND
2. TO THE FAR BLUE
 MOUNTAINS
3. THE DAYBREAKERS
4. SACKETT
5. LANDO
6. MOJAVE CROSSING
7. THE SACKETT
 BRAND
8. THE LONELY MEN
9. TREASURE
 MOUNTAIN
10. MUSTANG MAN
11. GALLOWAY
12. THE SKY-LINERS
13. THE MAN FROM THE
 BROKEN HILLS
14. RIDE THE DARK
 TRAIL

*To all the pioneers whose
journals and letters have done
so much to provide me with material*

Chapter 1

They could call it running away if they wanted to, but it made no sense to kill a man, or risk being killed over something so trivial. He had never used a gun against a man, and did not intend to begin now.

He glanced back, but the town lay far behind him, and there seemed to be no reason for pursuit.

Dawn would be breaking soon, and they would be expecting him on the street to face Dutch Akin, and Dutch would certainly be there, right in the middle of that Las Vegas street, a gun ready to his hand.

It was a savage custom, a ridiculous custom. His mother had been right to take him away from it, back to the eastern city where her family lived. She had never loved the West . . . not really.

He had been a fool to come west, even on business. But how could he have imagined he would run into trouble? Though he rarely took a drink, and was not inclined to argue, he had taken a drink while waiting for either Pearsall or Sparrow, and he had gotten into an argument. All right . . . he *had* made a mistake, but how was he to know they would make so much out of so little?

To hell with Dutch Akin, and with Las Vegas! He would be damned if he'd get himself killed over a few careless words in a saloon. It made no sense—no sense at all.

What would they say when they realized he was gone? When he failed to appear? At the thought, his ears reddened and he felt uncomfortable.

To hell with them! It was better to be a live coward than a dead hero.

Coward . . . the word rankled. Was he a coward? Had he been afraid? He searched himself for an

1

answer, and found none. He did not believe he was a coward. He had come away to avoid a ridiculous situation . . . or was he just telling himself that? Was he not actually afraid?

He seemed to feel his father's eyes upon him—those cool, thoughtful eyes that knew so well how to measure a man and judge what he had in him.

He remembered his father, the day they brought him home on a shutter, still alive, but badly shot up. There had been three men. One of them had taken a drink, waved a bottle, and staggered, but when Borden Chantry had come to arrest him the man suddenly dropped his bottle and two other men stepped from ambush, and his father had gone down in a wicked crossfire. He got off one shot, that was all. The three men had then fled the town.

His father had lived for two days in considerable pain before the doctor arrived from the fort; by the time he got there his father was dead.

It was as his mother had told him: if you lived by the gun you died by the gun.

But he remembered overhearing someone say as they left the cemetery, "I'd hate to be in their boots when Tom Chantry grows up!"

His father had been a cattleman, reasonably successful by any man's standards, but then had come the great freeze-up, and when the snow melted his father was a poor man, and so were a lot of others. Cattlemen could always get credit, and when they sold their herds they paid up; only Pa had no herd to sell.

The men of the town respected him, knew he had a family to feed, and they also knew that he was a man good with a gun, so they offered him the job of town marshal.

For six years he ran the town, and kept it free of serious trouble. He rarely had to draw his gun, and several times he held his fire to give the other man a chance to drop his, and they usually did—all but one. That man elected to fire . . . and missed. Borden Chantry did not miss.

That was the shooting that led to his death, for the men who came up the trail to kill him were friends of the dead man, and they staged the ambush that wiped out Borden Chantry.

It did no good to remember all that. Tom Chantry touched his horse with a spur. It would soon be light and he wanted to be far away before they discovered he was gone. He had been a fool to come west in the first place. Both Ma and Doris had tried to talk him out of it, but there was a shortage of beef in the East and he had argued with Earnshaw that they could buy it on the plains. No use dealing with a middleman.

Doris' father was Robert Earnshaw, a dealer in livestock in New York City. Lately he had branched out into real estate and banking, although livestock was still the backbone of his business. He had been quick to recognize the profit to be had if Tom Chantry could go west, buy cattle on the plains, and ship them east, and Tom had come west with his blessing.

Beef had been scarce in Kansas, but a cattleman told him of a herd that was being held outside of Las Vegas, Nevada, that still might be had. The owners, Pearsall and Sparrow, had been holding the cattle to speculate, but now were in a bind for money. Tom Chantry had immediately left for Las Vegas, sending a message ahead to make the appointment with the prospective sellers.

He had registered at the hotel and gone at once to the saloon where cattlemen were known to gather, and where Sparrow had said they would meet. While he waited, he had a drink.

Dutch Akin had come in, bumping him hard as he lurched up to the bar, then turning to glare at him with a muttered reference to a "dude."

Tom Chantry ignored the rudeness, although he felt irritation mounting within him. He edged over a little without seeming to do so, giving Akin more room. He knew he should go, but he had come all this way to see Sparrow, and the man was expected. It was simple courtesy for him to wait . . . so he waited.

Chantry had finished his drink, hesitated, then ordered another. He had not eaten since early that morning and knew that he should not have that second drink, but he was embarrassed to stay at the bar without ordering.

By the time he had finished his drink Sparrow had not come, so he started to turn away from the bar. Without warning a rough hand grasped his shoulder.

Suddenly furious, Chantry turned around sharply. Akin was grinning at him. "Dude, diden you hyar me? I invited you to drink wi'me."

"Sorry, I didn't hear, but I've had enough, thank you."

" 'I've had enough, thank you.' " Akin put his hand on his hip and aped the words in a falsetto; then his voice changed. "I'll tell you when you've had enough! Now belly up to the bar an' drink!"

"No."

The room was quiet. Every eye was on them. The drunken man suddenly seemed to be no longer drunk. "When Dutch Akin invites a man to drink, he damn well better drink," Akin said evenly. "You drink, mister."

"No."

It was foolish. A ridiculous situation. Tom Chantry was irritated with himself for remaining long enough to get involved, but there was no help for it now.

"I am sorry, my friend, but I have no wish for another drink. I was just leaving."

"You'll leave when I get damn good an' ready for you to leave. Now belly up to the bar."

Chantry merely glanced at him, then turned to leave the room. Again he felt the hand touch his shoulder, and this time his reaction was swift. He swung around quickly and, throwing his left hand back, took hold of the grasping arm and jerked hard.

Dutch Akin hit the floor with a crash, and as he realized what had been done to him his hand swept back for his gun.

"*Dutch!*" The sharp voice cut through the haze of anger in Dutch Akin's brain.

A short, slender man in a business suit and a white hat was holding a gun in his hand. "The gentleman isn't armed, Dutch. If you haven't noticed that, you'd better. You draw that gun and I'll put a hole into you."

"This ain't none of your affair, Sparrow. This is just me and him."

Sparrow? Chantry turned his head to look. A man of about forty-five, well-dressed, cool, competent-looking. This was the man he had come to see.

"It is any man's affair as long as this gentleman is not wearing a gun. If you shoot an unarmed man you'll hang for it, Dutch. I'll see that you do."

Dutch got up slowly, holstering his pistol. "All right," he said calmly. "All right, Sparrow. But I'll be on the street at daybreak wearin' this gun, and he better be armed, because if he ain't I'll break both his legs."

Dutch turned sharply and walked from the room.

Chantry held out his hand. "Tom Chantry here, Mr. Sparrow. Thank you—thank you very much."

They walked back to the hotel together. "Bad case, that Akin," Sparrow commented, "a real trouble-maker. But he's good with a gun, so be careful."

Chantry shrugged. "I doubt if I ever see him again. Actually, *you* are the man I came to see. I understand you have a herd of beef outside of town that you might sell."

"I might." They had reached the deserted porch of the hotel. Sparrow bit the end from a cigar. "But you are mistaken if you think Akin won't show. The man may be a trouble-maker and a loud-mouth, but he's got sand, and he's killed a man or two. You can expect him."

"It's absurd, Mr. Sparrow. The whole affair was uncalled for. He will have forgotten all about it in the morning."

Sparrow lighted his cigar, threw the match into the dust, and then spoke around the cigar. "No, Mr. Chantry, he will not have forgotten it. Nor will anyone else. Come hell or high water, Dutch Akin will be in the street tomorrow, and if you don't own a pistol you had better buy or borrow one. You'll need it."

"Are you seriously suggesting that I be out there in the street? That I engage in a duel with this—this ape?"

Sparrow glanced at him. "Are you by any chance related to Borden Chantry?"

"I am his son."

"Then I would think—"

Suddenly, Tom Chantry was impatient. "Mr. Sparrow, I came to Las Vegas to see you, to make you an offer for your cattle. The firm I represent, Earnshaw and Company, is an eastern firm, and until now we have done our business through others. We've hoped to set up some business connections out here and buy cattle at the source. We had hoped to buy your herd. I did not come out here to be involved in brawls or shootings, or anything of that sort. I dislike violence, and will have nothing to do with this affair."

"I see."

Sparrow's manner had grown cool. "I knew your father," he said after a minute, "and I respected him. I was not interested in selling cattle at this time, and we're holding them on good grass so there is no need. However, I thought that the son of Borden Chantry and I might strike a bargain."

"And we are ready, sir."

"You went east soon after your father's death, didn't you?"

"Yes, sir."

"The situation back east is very different from out here, Mr. Chantry. Money is not always the only consideration. Out here we place emphasis upon the basic virtues, and I have noticed that the more organized our lives become the less attention we pay to such things as courage and loyalty. Organization seems to eliminate the necessity for such things, but out here they are the very stuff of life."

"And what does that mean?"

"Simply this: that a man's courage or lack of it is a matter of economic importance in the West. There are few ventures that can be attempted out here where courage is not a necessity, and anyone engaged in such a venture has a right to know the courage of those who are to share the risk."

"What you are saying is that if I do not meet Dutch Akin tomorrow I had better go back east?"

"Exactly that. We will agree the circumstances are disagreeable, but such things cannot be avoided, and you have no choice."

"I don't believe that."

Sparrow shrugged. "It does not matter what you believe. Your father understood, and he lived by the code."

"And died by it."

"That sometimes happens."

"Then," Tom Chantry replied quietly, "I am in the wrong country. I have no desire to kill . . . or to be killed. I shall go to Dutch Akin and apologize."

"He will despise you."

"Very well, but that will be the end of it."

Sparrow drew on his cigar, then took it from his mouth as though it suddenly had a bad taste. "No, Mr. Chantry, that will not be the end. It will be only the beginning. The bullies will know you are fair game, that you will not fight, and therefore are to be bullied with impunity. The decent people will simply ignore you, the bullies will hunt you down, and some of them will keep on pushing just to see how much you can take before you do fight.

"Understand this, Mr. Chantry, the love of peace and the unwillingness to fight never kept anyone out of trouble."

They left it at that, but during the night Tom Chantry made his decision.

Turning now in the saddle, he looked back again. There was nothing—nothing at all.

All around were the vast sky and the open prairie. To the north there were mountains, ahead was a broken, rugged country. It was not until then that he realized what he had done.

He had ridden west, not east.

Chapter 2

To the east lay home, friends, security from all this. His mother and Doris were in the East, his job and his future were there. Yet he had ridden west. Why?

What impulse had caused him to turn west when east was the logical direction? Was there some urge within him to avoid security? To avoid escape?

His choice back there had been simple. To use a gun, or not to use it.

He did not think he had actually been afraid, but how was he to know? Sparrow's attitude could be that of everyone west of the Mississippi, and of many of those east of it. Such a story would get around, of course, and even those who commended him for good judgment would suspect his courage.

By turning west he had escaped nothing but the immediate meeting with Dutch Akin, for the situation might arise again. If so, would he run again? How often could he run?

But that was not the important thing now. He had come west to buy cattle that could be shipped east. If he could not get them in Las Vegas he must find them elsewhere, and that meant he might ride north to the Wyoming country and ship over the Union Pacific.

Earnshaw had advanced the money for his trip west, and he carried a draft against Earnshaw's bank with which to pay for the cattle. It was his duty to complete the business that had brought him here; Earnshaw was depending on him.

Tom Chantry considered the situation. Santa Fe lay to the west, not over three days' ride, he believed. It was doubtful if the required cattle could be found there; and if found they must be driven to the railhead, which meant a drive through Las Vegas—something he could not consider at this time.

8

His logical course was to strike north, but first he must have bedding, supplies, and a pack horse.

The horse he had purchased at the livery stable seemed a good one, and Tom Chantry was an experienced judge of horseflesh. He had bought and sold stock for Earnshaw long enough to be.

Ahead of him lay the stage station at Kearney's Gap; lights showed in the windows, although the sky was gray with dawn's first light. He turned his mount and rode up to the hitch rack.

Behind the house he heard the squeak and complaint of a windlass. He walked to the edge of the porch and looked past the corner. A man with rumpled hair, his suspenders hanging loose, had just drawn a bucket of water.

"Howdy!" he said cheerfully. "Coffee's on. Be fryin' eggs. Come in an' set."

How much time did he have? Traveling would begin at daybreak, and the stage would be coming from Las Vegas shortly after. He did not want to be here when it arrived.

Over coffee he spoke of Santa Fe and Socorro.

"If'n you're headin' for Socorro now," the stage tender said, "you're headin' right. But a man who wanted to get to Santa Fe a-horseback is a plumb fool to ride the trail. Right yonder"—he pointed—"is a good horseback or pack trail across the mountains. Rougher, but a whole sight shorter. Thisaway you swing south and take a big bend. No need. You headin' for Santa Fe?"

"Socorro," Chantry said, "but I'm traveling light. You haven't got any trade goods, have you?"

"A mite. Sell some of the Injuns once in a while. What was you needin'?"

Less than half an hour later, with two blankets, a sack of grub, and a bowie knife to cut firewood, Chantry headed west. When out of sight of the station he turned abruptly from the road and cut back into the brush to find the other trail.

He found it at Agua Zarca and followed it toward the crossing of the Tecolote at San Geronimo. Without leaving the saddle, he removed his coat, stripped off his white shirt, and donned a dark red shirt bought at the stage station. Then he tied his coat behind his saddle.

At noon, well back in the scattered piñons, he un-saddled, watered his horse at a seep, made coffee, and ate a couple of dry biscuits.

Slowly, the tension left him. The smell of the piñons and juniper, the coolness and quiet of the day, the slow circling of far-off buzzards, the cloud shadows on the hills began to soak into his being and left him rested and at peace. When he mounted up and started on once more, he was at one with the land.

His first desire had been to get away from Las Vegas, but now that he was away he knew his best bet would have been to ride north toward Mora and thence to Cimarron, where there would be a lot of cattle.

He reached the Santa Fe Trail again near Glorieta, skirted Santa Fe, and took the trail for Taos. The way he had left Las Vegas rankled. He did not like being considered a coward, and he did not believe he was one, but a good many people would believe so.

But that was behind him. Once in Cimarron, he would buy the cattle, drive them to the railhead, and within a few hours after that he would be on his way back to Doris.

Doris . . .

He took his time. He camped when the mood was on him, and rode on again when he grew restless; when possible, he avoided the main trail.

He was somewhere south of E-Town when he heard the horse. It was coming fast, and he pulled over to be out of the way.

The horse was a blaze-faced roan, and it was carry-ing double. The riders pulled up when they saw him.

"Howdy there, stranger! Comin' fer?"

"Santa Fe," he replied.

They were young, rough-looking, and one man had a bandaged arm.

"See many folks on the trail?"

"Nobody."

"You'll likely see some. By this time there's a-plenty of folks headin' our way. We was in a shootin' back yonder in Elizabethtown. Hank got himself winged and got his hoss kilt right under him. Good hoss, too."

"Bud," Hank said, "you notice somethin' peculiar? This gent ain't wearin' no gun."

"Rough country," Bud commented. "If'n I was you, mister, I'd wear a gun. You never know who you'll meet up with."

Chantry shrugged. "I don't wear a gun. If you'll pardon my saying so, I think guns lead to trouble."

"You hear that, Bud? He ain't wearin' no gun."

"Maybe guns do lead to trouble," Bud said seriously, "but they's times when not wearin' one will." Suddenly he held a pistol. "Git down off that hoss, mister."

"Now see here! I—"

"You git down off that hoss or I'll shoot you off, an' I ain't goin' to tell you again."

Hank was grinning at him, his lean, unshaven face taunting. "He'll do it, too, stranger. Bud here's kilt four men. He's one up on me."

"There's no need for this," Chantry said. "I've done you no harm."

He felt the sting of the nicked ear and then heard the blast of the pistol, although probably everything happened at once—the stab of flame, the report, the flash of pain from his ear.

"Mister, I ain't a-talkin' just to hear the wind blow. You git down."

Slowly, carefully, Tom Chantry swung down from his horse. Inwardly he was seething, but he was frightened, too. The man had meant to kill him.

Hank quickly dropped from his seat in back of Bud and swung up on Chantry's horse. With a wild, derisive yell they rode off, and he stood in the trail staring after them.

The place where they had come upon him was among scattered trees, but before him the country opened wide. It was high, lonely country, and ice still lay in the lake beside the trail. As far as he could see there was nothing—no house, no animal, no man. But he was alive. Had he been wearing a gun they might have killed him . . . or he might have killed one of them.

An hour later he was still alone, still in wide, open country, but he seemed to be a little nearer the mountains that rimmed the high basin.

That man had not missed by intention. He had wanted to kill. He had meant to kill. It was a shocking thing, an unreal thing. Chantry had held no weapon, had made no threatening gesture, and yet the men who had stolen his horse and his outfit would have killed him . . . and could have.

Would they have robbed him had he been armed? His mind refused to acknowledge the thought, but there was that doubt, that uncertainty. Had he been armed they might have tried to get the drop on him, to take his gun, and then rob him.

Suddenly he saw a thin, distant spiral of dust. It drew nearer and nearer, dissolved into a dozen hard-riding men. They drew up, the dust swirling around them.

"Did you see two men?" one of them asked. "Two men on one horse?"

"They are on two horses now. They stole mine at gun point."

"You mean you let 'em have it? Those were the Talrim boys . . . they murdered a man back yonder, and it ain't the first."

"I had no choice. I wasn't armed."

They stared at him. The bearded man shrugged. "This here's no country to travel without a weapon." He turned in his saddle. "Tell you what you do." He pointed. "Over the hill yonder—maybe three miles—there's a shack and a corral. You'll find a couple of horses there.

"You take one of them and ride on to Cimarron. Leave a note on the table in there . . . that's the Andress cabin and the old man will understand. You can leave the horse for him in Cimarron, or just turn him loose. He'll go home."

And then they were gone, and he was alone on the road, with the dust of the posse drifting around him.

It was coming on to sundown when he reached the Andress cabin and caught up one of the horses he found there. There was no saddle, but he had ridden bareback before this. He twisted a hackamore from some rope and mounted up.

Then, remembering the note, he swung down, tied the horse, and went inside the cabin. It was still and bare—a table, two chairs, a bunk in a corner, a few dog-eared magazines, and some old books. It was neat, everything was in its place.

He sat down and, searching in vain for paper, finally took an envelope from his pocket and scratched a brief note on the back with a pencil he carried. He weighted the note down with a silver dollar to pay for the use of the horse, pulled the door shut after him, mounted again, and rode out on the trail to Cimarron.

His face itched and, putting up a hand, he found there was dried blood from the nicked ear. He rubbed it away, then felt gingerly of the ear. The bleeding had stopped, but the ear was very tender. Moistening his handkerchief at his lips, he carefully wiped the dried blood away from the ear.

That had been a narrow escape. It was pure luck that the shot had not killed him, and pure whim on the part of Bud Talrim that he had not fired a second shot to better effect.

Tom Chantry shuddered . . . it was the same sudden reaction one has that usually draws the remark, "Somebody just stepped on your grave."

He might have been dead, and he might have been robbed, leaving no identification, with nothing to tell who he was or why he was here. It was appalling to consider how close he had come to an utterly useless death and a nameless grave. Back home nobody would ever have known what happened to him.

He made his decision then. He was going to get out of this country, and he was going to get out by the first stage, the very first train. He was going back east and he was going to stay there and live in a civilized community.

Since the shocking death of his father there had been no violence in his life. He had grown up first in a small New England village, going to school, fishing along the streams, hunting rabbits, squirrels, and then deer. He had gone to church, and had taken for granted the well-dressed, quiet-talking people, the neat streets, the well-ordered little town.

He had been aware of the town officials, the local constable, and the talk of courts and trials. He knew the town had a jail, although it was rarely occupied by more than an occasional drunk. Later, in New York, the police had been more obvious. There were fire companies, and workmen to repair damage to the streets.

With these memories in his mind, he had also been conscious now for several minutes of the drum of a horse's hoofs on the trail behind him. He turned to see a rider on a bay horse—the very bay he had seen in the Andress corral when he caught up the horse he was riding. The rider was a tall, straight old man with a white mustache and clear blue eyes.

"Howdy, Chantry!" he called. "I'm Luke Andress. No need to leave that dollar. In this country if a man needs a horse all he needs to do is let a body know."

"Thank you." Briefly, Tom Chantry explained.

"Murderers," Andress said; "savages. But you ought to carry a gun. If you'd had a gun they'd never have tried it . . . not to your face, anyway. Those Talrims are back-shootin' murderers. At least, those two are."

"Do you think the posse will catch them?"

"Them? No, they won't—not by a durned sight. Those Talrims are a bad lot, but they're mountain men. With two horses under them and what grub you had they'll lose themselves in the mountains west of here. They're better than Injuns when it comes to runnin' an' hidin'."

Andress glanced at him. "You figuring on ranchin' it?"

"No, I came out to buy cattle, and after what's happened in the last few days I can't get out of here fast enough."

Andress was silent as they rode on for a short distance, and then he said, "It's a good country, Chantry. It's like any country when it's young and growin'. It attracts the wild spirits, the loose-footed. Some of them settle down and become mighty good citizens, but there's always the savages. You have 'em back east, too."

"Not like here."

"Just like here . . . only you've got an organized society, a police department, and law courts. The bad actor there knows he ain't goin' to get far if he starts cuttin' up. Folks won't stand for it. But you walk down the street back there and you can figure maybe two out of every five folks you pass are savages. They may not even know it themselves, but once the law breaks down you'd find out fast enough. First they'd prey on the peaceful ones, then on each other . . . it's jungle law, boy, and don't you forget it.

"Out here there's nothin' but local law, and a man can be as mean as he wants to until folks catch up with him, or until he meets some bigger, tougher man. This is raw country; the good folks are good because it's their nature, and the bad can run to meanness until somebody fetches them up the short. That's why you'd better arm yourself. If you're goin' to be in this country you'll need a gun."

"Guns lead to trouble."

"Well," Andress said dryly, "I can see where not havin' a gun led you to trouble." He paused a moment. "The thieves and the killers are goin' to have guns, so if the honest men don't have 'em they just make it easier for the vicious. But you hold to your way of thinkin', boy, if you've a mind to. It's your way, and you got a right to it."

Cimarron showed up ahead, lights appearing, although it was not yet dark.

"Go to the St. James," Andress said. "There are some cattlemen there almost every night. They come in to play cards, or to set around and talk. You'll find some cattle, but if you're not goin' to carry a gun you'd better talk soft and stay clear of whiskey."

A room, a bath, and a good dinner made a lot of difference. Tom Chantry stood before the mirror and combed his dark hair, then he straightened his tie and shrugged his coat into a neater set on his shoulders.

Now for business . . . a thousand head of steers and the crew to drive them to the railhead. With any kind of luck he could be on the train for New York within a matter of a few days.

The saloon at the St. James was not crowded, for the hour was early, but it was at this hour that most of the business was conducted by the clientele. The western saloon, Tom Chantry knew, was more than merely a drinking room; it was a clearing house for information as to trails, grazing conditions, Indian attitudes, and business and political considerations generally.

At the bar Tom introduced himself to Henry Lambert, who owned the St. James. Lambert had once been chef at the White House, brought there originally by Grant, for he had cooked for Grant during part of the war.

"I am interested in buying cattle, Mr. Lambert. My name is Tom Chantry. If you know of anyone—"

"Mr. Chantry"—Lambert's face had stiffened slightly at the name—"I do know of cattle that might be for sale, but I would not advise you to buy them."

Surprised, Tom turned toward him. "Would you mind telling me why? Buying cattle is why I came to Cimarron."

"Mr. Chantry, I am a Frenchman, but I have become acquainted with the customs here. To buy the cattle would be easy, but you must get them to the railroad. I do not believe you could hire the men to do it."

"You mean there aren't any? At this time of year?"

"There are men, but they would not work for you, Mr. Chantry. I hope you will not take offense, for I am only telling you what is true. You see, there are no secrets in the West, and there has been talk, here in this bar, about how you failed to meet Dutch Akin."

"But what has that to do with hiring a crew?"

"Mr. Chantry, it is a long, hard drive from here to the end of the track. Much of it is through country where roving bands of Cheyenne, Comanche, and Kiowa may be found, and the Arapahoes too, I think. It is a hard country, without much water, with danger of sandstorms, stampedes, and other troubles. Men do not want to trust themselves to the leadership of a man whose courage is in question."

Tom Chantry felt himself turn cold. He stared at the cup of coffee before him for several minutes before he spoke. "Mr. Lambert," he said finally, "I am not a coward. I simply do not believe in carrying guns, and I do not believe in killing."

Lambert shrugged. "I do not believe in killing either, and yet a dozen men have died in this very room, died with guns in their hands.*

"There is too much killing, yet the fact remains, that we live in a wild country, and one relatively lawless; and no man is willing to attempt a cattle drive that may demand the utmost in courage, with a man whose courage is suspect."

When Chantry spoke his voice was hoarse. "Thank you, Mr. Lambert," he said.

He sat alone, staring at the coffee as it grew cold in the cup.

---

*Actually 26 men are said to have been killed in that room during the wild days.

For an hour they talked. Bone McCarthy was a creek knowledgeable man with much experience on cattle drives and roundups. He ran through the possible rules one by one. Bad horses, stampedes, maybe a rattle-

Chapter 3

After a short time the depression left him. He would not be defeated. If there were cattle for sale he meant to buy them and, somehow or other, get them to market.

Luckily the Talrim boys had not thought to rob him of anything but his horse and his outfit. That was what they needed, and the thought of going through his pockets had not occurred to them. He still had his letter of credit and the money he had been carrying.

He was considering his next move when Luke Andress came over to the table, carrying a beer. "Mind if I sit down?"

"Please do."

"Had any luck?"

"No. And from what Lambert tells me I couldn't get the hands to drive a herd if I bought one."

"So what are you goin' to do?"

He considered that for a moment, and then said, "Mr. Andress, I am going to buy cattle, and I am going to drive them through if I have to do it myself . . . alone."

Andress chuckled. "You may have to, but I'll tell you what. See that big gent over there at the bar? The one with the elk's tooth on his watch chain? He's got maybe five or six hundred head you could buy. Lee Dauber has eight or nine hundred head. I think you can dicker for 'em."

"Thanks."

"Now here's another thing. See that tall, good-lookin' fellow at the table yonder? That's French Williams. He'd sell you beef . . . he'll have seven or eight hundred head, but you'd better leave 'em alone."

"Why?"

"French is a mighty peculiar man. He's a smilin', easy-talkin', friendly man . . . almighty friendly. He

18

sells a lot of beef, one time or another. He must have some uncommonly good bulls, because judgin' by the amount of beef he sells each cow must be havin' three calves."

"I don't want any brands that could be questioned."

"Nobody will question French's brand. Anyway, he never puts a brand on anything that's ever been branded before."

Andress turned his beer stein on the table and said, "Boy, I don't know why, but I like you. What I've told you about French could get me killed."

"I won't repeat it."

They sat silent for several minutes and then Tom Chantry said, "I know what I am going to do."

"What?"

"I'm going to buy cattle from those men if they will sell, and then I am going to hire French Williams to take them through for me."

Luke Andress stared at him, then began to chuckle. "Boy, you've got nerve, I'll say that for you! But you be careful of French! He won't go into any deal unless he figures to come out ahead."

There was no use wasting time. If the word had gotten around, they all knew he had backed out of a fight with Dutch Akin, and the only thing left for him was either to skip the country or take the bull by the horns. He got up, excused himself to Andress, and walked across the room.

Two men sat with French Williams, and they all looked up when he stopped at their table.

"French Williams? I am Tom Chantry."

French looked up lazily. "I've heard of you."

"Then they have told you that I backed down for Dutch Akin. The simple facts of the case are that I haven't time to go around shooting every Tom, Dick, and Harry who wants to get drunk and start a fight. I came here to buy cattle. I hear that you and some of these other gentlemen have cattle for sale. I've also been told that I'll never be able to hire a crew to take my herd to the railhead. But I don't believe it.

"I want to buy what cattle you have for sale, and I'll pay cash for them. I will also buy whatever cattle are for sale by any of the other gentlemen in this room on the same terms."

"And how do you figure to get them to market?" French had scarcely moved. He was sitting back in his chair, staring up at Chantry, cool and calculating, almost insolent.

"I have been told by various people that you are a shrewd dealer, and that you are not to be trusted." His voice was loud enough for others to hear, and they were all listening. "I have heard that anybody who gets into a cattle deal with you will lose his eyeteeth. I don't believe it."

French Williams' expression had tightened a little as Chantry talked, but his eyes had never left Tom's face.

"You don't?"

"No, I do not. That is why I am offering you one-third of the sale price of the herd if you will drive my cattle to the railhead."

For a moment there was silence in the saloon, and then French Williams chuckled. "Sit down," he said. "I want to buy you a drink."

"All right, and I'll buy you one."

Chantry sat down, and Williams' black eyes glinted with amusement.

"You don't think I'll rook you?"

"No. I think you're a man of your word."

French eyed him curiously. "You're either a damn fool or you're pretty smart. Well, we'll see who's smart and who isn't. You think I'm honest and I think you've got sand, so I'll tell you what I'll do.

"I will take your herd to the railhead for expenses . . . if you will come with us and stay all the way through. If you don't stay with it, I take it all . . . every last steer."

French was smiling, his black eyes taunting.

"That's the deal. Take it or leave it."

Chantry pushed the bottle toward him. "Pour your drink, French. We're in business."

"You'll take it?"

"Of course."

Chantry turned toward the bar. "Mr. Dauber? Let's talk about cattle."

Lee Dauber walked over to the table, a glass in his hand. "I can deliver. How do I know you can pay?"

Tom Chantry placed his letter of credit on the table. "There it is."

Dauber dismissed it with a gesture. "A piece of paper. I go by a man's word. You backed down for Dutch Akin. How do I know your word is good?"

French Williams looked up. "Lee? *I* say his word is good. Any argument?"

Lee Dauber shrugged. "Your funeral, French. All right, we'll dicker. I've got a thousand head, give or take a few."

For an hour the talk went on, and at the end of it Tom Chantry held title to twenty-two hundred head of cattle, stock for which he had paid with sums drawn from his letter of credit. Of the money behind that letter of credit only a little of it was his own; the remainder belonged to Earnshaw and Company.

With luck the drive would take them thirty days, perhaps a bit more or less; and if he made it through, he would have a herd whose price would not be less than fifty thousand dollars, of which two-thirds would be sheer profit. On the other hand, if he failed he would lose everything, and Earnshaw would take a heavy loss.

He was guessing on the time it would take to get the herd to the railhead, for he had never made a drive with cattle, although he knew something of the problems involved. Moreover, the railroad was moving west . . . he was not sure French Williams knew that, and he did not intend to tell him.

The railroad had been stalled at Dodge City for several years because of the financial depression and the inability to raise money for the investment. Now the rails had started moving again, and when he left the railroad he had been assured they could hold to a speed of about a mile a day, laying track. That might be optimistic . . . what he was going to need was information, information for himself alone.

There was always the chance of some casual traveler relaying the knowledge, for it was certainly no secret, but rumors had been flying during all the time since construction stopped, and many western men had simply given up believing anything until they saw it.

Alone that night in his room, Tom Chantry stretched out on his bed, hands clasped behind his head, and thought the thing through.

He was under no illusions about French Williams. The man was hard as nails and dangerous as a rattler, but he was a man of fierce pride, and Chantry knew he had touched it when he called him a man of his word.

Obviously French was a gambler. It was a game of winner-take-all, and French was not the kind of man to enjoy losing. What he was gambling on was, in essence, Chantry's staying quality. Tom Chantry was no fool, and he knew that French Williams would make it very rough.

Did Williams believe him a coward? That remained to be seen. More likely than not he had no thoughts on the matter, and cared less. He would test Chantry's nerve with sadistic pleasure . . . and would be an interested observer of Chantry's reactions.

Actually, French Williams was risking only his time. And he might like a ride to Dodge anyway. The risk was all for Tom Chantry; the gain, if he won, would be great. But had he any right to take such a risk with another man's money?

They needed beef badly if they were to continue operations as planned. Tom Chantry considered the gamble he had taken and admitted, reluctantly, that he had been foolish. He had been challenged, and like any green kid he had accepted the challenge.

Now he must plan. He must try to foresee what French would do. The most obvious thing was the old western trick of giving him a bad horse to ride, and this he had every right to expect. It was usual for any tenderfoot on a cow ranch or a cattle drive to be given a bad horse just as a joke.

Well, let them try. He had been riding horses since he was a child, and even back east he had never quit riding. He had handled some pretty bad ones, but he doubted that he had tangled with anything like what they could give him out here, and he was sure they were even now planning on that.

He knew it was going to be rough, especially as he

had taken water for Dutch Akin. No cowhand would consider that anything but cowardice, and they would have nothing but contempt for him.

At daybreak he was up, and after a quick breakfast he went to the livery stable and bought two horses. Both were tough and well-seasoned, and he paid premium prices for them. He bargained, but the horse dealer knew he wanted horses and knew what he wanted them for. He got good horses, and the price he finally paid was not as bad as he had expected. One was a line-back dun, the other a blue roan, both bigger than the usual cow horse, but agile enough. The dun was an excellent cutting horse, the blue roan was fair; both had the look of possessing staying quality. "Which I'd better have myself," he said to himself.

He bought a used saddle, a blanket, and all the essential gear. At the general store he bought a slicker, a bedroll, and a little other equipment.

"You better have yourself a gun," the storekeeper suggested.

Chantry shook his head, smiling. "I doubt if I'll need it. I will have a Winchester, though. I've never killed a buffalo, and we might need the meat."

He bought a Winchester '73 and four hundred rounds of ammunition. "If I am going to use this," he commented, "I'd better have some practice."

"Better not try it near a cattle herd," the storekeeper said dryly, "or you'll have a stampede."

They all thought him a tenderfoot, he reflected, and in one sense it was true, but he was western-born and a lot had soaked in that stayed with him. One did not live in the environment during the impressionable years and not retain something from it.

His father had been a man who talked of his work and his life, and he was a man who had known men and stock, who had pioneered in wild country. Had he been trying, even then, to instruct his son? After all, what did a father have to pass on to his children but his own personal reaction to the world? Of what use was experience if one could not pass on at least a little of what one had learned?

For the first time Tom Chantry thought of that, and

suddenly he was seeing his father in a new light. Like
many another son, he had failed to understand the true
nature of the man who was his father until he himself
began to cope with the problems of which life is made
up.

They were to make their gather and pool the cattle
on the Vermejo River, east and a bit north of Cimarron,
and their drive would begin from there.

He would go there and join them. He would ride his
own horses, but if they suggested a bad one, he would
try it. He could be thrown, but he could also get
back on. Tom Chantry decided he knew what to expect,
and he was prepared for it. The trouble was, he did not
know French Williams.

He knew little enough about the Vermejo River.
Only that it began somewhere in the Sangre de Cristos
and flowed down from the mountains, across the old
Santa Fe Trail to lose itself, so far as he knew, somewhere in the open country beyond.

Riding the blue roan and leading the dun, he started
for the camp on the Vermejo. He told himself he was
ready for anything, and he was still telling himself that
when he spotted the camp under some cottonwoods.

There was already a good gathering of cattle, and he
could see various riders bringing in more. He passed
near one rider, a tall, lean man with red hair, but the
rider seemed not to notice him, although Chantry spoke.

He rode up to the chuck wagon and swung down.
French Williams was leaning back against his bedroll,
smiling. And it was not a pleasant smile. It was taunting, challenging, showing, something that might be contempt, and might be curiosity. As Tom Chantry walked
forward and started to speak, a man came from behind the chuck wagon. He stepped out and stopped,
waiting.

The man was Dutch Akin.

Chapter 4

For a moment all action was suspended. Tom Chantry could feel the heavy pounding of his heart, and his mouth was dry, but when he spoke his voice was clear and steady. "Hello, Dutch. Want some coffee?"

This was what Chantry had not expected, yet it was what he might have expected from French Williams. And it was an indication of the extent to which Williams was prepared to go.

"Don't mind if I do," Dutch said.

Chantry picked up the pot and filled Dutch's cup, then his own. "Sorry about the other night, Dutch," he said, "but I had no reason to kill you, and I had no wish to die."

Dutch shrugged uncomfortably. Sober, he was not a belligerent man, nor was he given to talk. If you had a job to do, you did it. If you had a man to shoot, you shot him. But talking about it made him uneasy, wanting to be away and finished with it. " 'S all right," he said, gulping the coffee. "I got no argument with you."

French Williams sat up. If he was disappointed it did not show, and Tom Chantry doubted that he was. It had been in the nature of an experiment, and had they killed each other he would have been no more disturbed.

Chantry indicated the cattle. "They're in good shape. Some of your stuff?"

"Uh-huh," French said. "They've been held in the high meadows where there's lots of good grama." He glanced toward the horses. "I see you got yourself some horses. Two won't be enough, you know."

Chantry's expression was bland. "I had an idea you'd already selected some mounts for me, French, so I only bought two."

"You'd ride a horse I'd pick for you?"

"Why not? Well, let's just say I'd try."

The other hands who had been loafing about, obviously to see what would happen when he met Dutch Akin, now drifted off about their work. Tom Chantry drank his coffee slowly, studying the various men, watching the work, and enjoying the brief respite from what was to come.

He was no cowhand and would not attempt to compete with them on their own ground. He could round up cattle, he could read brands, and so could make himself generally useful. He would not be an idler. It would be wise to move slowly at first, to see who could do what, and generally become acquainted.

He had gained no ground by facing Dutch. He had simply done what had to be done, and he knew the hands would be waiting to see what kind of a man he was—and most of them, he felt sure, had made up their minds about that.

As he watched the cattle the enormity of what he had undertaken slowly came over him. His own capital he was free to do with as he saw fit, but he had gambled a large sum that belonged to Earnshaw and Company. Therefore there was no choice. The herd must go through, and it must arrive in good shape and be sold to advantage . . . no matter what the cost to him.

Riders were bringing in small bunches of cattle from draws and breaks. Saddling the dun, he rode out and helped here and there, at the same time noting the brands. All of those being held had come from French Williams' own outfit. Some of the brands were fresh, but he saw no evidence of reworking.

At daybreak he was on the range with the others, and was there when Lee Dauber's cattle began to arrive. They came divided into three herds for easy handling, and Dauber moved them along at a good clip. These were big, rangy steers, older than most of Williams' stuff, and in not as good shape.

During the following days while the cattle were being brought together for the drive to the railhead, he worked hard, harder than he had ever worked before. He was up before the first streak of light in the morning sky, and tumbled into his bedroll when supper was over. With the others he stood night guard, and in many ways that came to be the best time.

Only three men rode night guard at a time, and they were scattered, meeting only at intervals as they rode around the sleeping herd. It was a time for thinking, a time for remembering. Yet, oddly, he rarely thought of Doris, and rarely of his home in the East. His thoughts kept reaching back into his boyhood, before his father was killed.

He remembered the hot, still hours in the town, walking barefooted up the dusty street, seeing the tall, still-faced men in boots and spurs sitting along the boardwalk in front of the hotel, or seeing them leaning on the corral bars, watching the horses.

The parched brown prairie, long without rain, the tumbleweeds rolling before the wind under dark, rain-filled clouds, the blue streaks of a distant rainstorm viewed from far off . . . the call of quail at sundown . . . his father washing his face and hands in the tin basin outside the kitchen door, sleeves rolled up, showing the white of his arms where the sun never reached.

He remembered the Indians who came to the ranch, squatting around near the corral, and his father feeding them, carrying the food to them himself . . . and the night the wounded brave had ridden up to the house, clinging one-handed to his horse's mane. That was on the old ranch, before Pa lost it in the big freeze . . . where had that ranch been, anyway? His memories were mostly from the later period when Pa was marshal.

They had gone back to the ranch once, all of them, driving in a buckboard. "There it is, Helen," Pa had said, "fifteen years of brutal hard work and a lot of dreams, all gone in one freeze."

Tom Chantry remembered the tall old cotton-woods around the house, the log cabin his father had built, then added to . . . the cold water from the hand-dug well. "I planned all this for you, Tom," his father had said, "but I reckoned without the snow and the cold."

The old ranch had been somewhere east of here, he
believed. A boy doesn't have much sense of location
when he is six.

Suddenly, he remembered The Hole. At least, that
was what he called it.

There had been a small spring about a mile from
the ranch, and he had ridden over there once when he
was about six. The spring came down from under an
overhang of rock, about two feet off the ground, and
the water fell into a rock basin, trickled over its lip and
down into the meadow below, where it was again swal-
lowed up.

Some dirt had fallen into the spring from one of the
overhanging banks, and he was scooping it out with his
hands when at the back of the spring where the water
ran down from the darkness under the rock, he saw The
Hole.

Actually, it was where the water came from, but the
opening was much bigger than the space taken up by the
trickle of water. Peering back into the deepest shadow,
he could see the hole was about three feet across and
almost that in height. He stood barefooted in the cold
water, and could look back into the hole, but could
make out nothing. Looking down at his feet, he could
just see the light across the water.

Evidently spring rains had shot out of the hole with
some force and had gradually worn the rock back until
there was space enough for a boy to stand. With a long
stick he poked into the darkness. There was a pool of
water where it trickled over the edge, but his stick
could not reach either wall or roof. Later, with a longer
stick he probed the darkness and succeeded in touching
rock on the right side of the stream. Overhead he
could find nothing, but there was a rock floor on the left
of the stream.

From outside there was no indication of anything
like the cave. There was only a dip in the prairie, a
natural runoff for water, and a slab of rock was exposed
from under which the water ran. Anyone stopping by
for a drink would suspect nothing. Although a man
might enter the opening once he knew of it, only a
child or a small animal would be likely to find it.

He named the place The Hole, and told his father about it.

All that was long ago . . . he had not thought of The Hole for twenty years that he could recall.

Tom Chantry gave no orders. If he saw anything that needed doing he did it himself, or reported it to French. He had no friends in the outfit, although French talked to him occasionally. Chantry was puzzled by him. Of French's background he knew nothing, but somehow the man gave him the impression that he had education, and a better background than most of the men in the outfit, but French volunteered nothing, and Tom Chantry knew better than to ask.

In general, the men ignored him. Oddly enough, when he did begin to make a friend it was Dutch Akin, of all people.

It began casually enough. He was riding back to the chuck wagon when he saw another rider following a route that would bring them together. Not until they were too close to turn aside did either recognize the other. It was Dutch.

"Beautiful country, Dutch," Chantry said.

Dutch merely grunted, then after a few minutes of silence he said, "You better not rest too easy. French is a holy terror. He's a good man to work for, gen'rally speakin', but he'd rather stir up trouble than eat. You let down one minute an' he'll be all over you."

"Thanks. He's not an easy man to understand."

"That he ain't," Dutch agreed dryly, "but he knows cows and no man alive is better on a trail than him." Then he said, "Mr. Chantry, I ain't one to stick my nose in, but if we all come up to trouble, you'd best run it. French will shoot you right into a range war . . . he's quick and he goes hog-wild an' mean. I've seen it."

"Thanks again." The horses walked a dozen yards before Chantry spoke again. "Dutch, do you think I'm yellow? I'm asking a question, not trying to invite a fight."

Dutch grinned, and then he said soberly, "No, I don't think nothin' of the kind. I might have. But not after the way you come up to me back there. I'd say you used better judgment than me back in Las Vegas.

"The only thing is," he added, "you not carryin' a gun makes a lot of them think you're scared . . . and believe me, it won't keep you out of trouble."

"But we're both alive, Dutch."

"Uh-huh, and if it wasn't for you one of us would be dead, but that cuts no ice. You just plain lucked out with the Talrim boys . . . they'd shoot you soon as look at you."

When they rode into camp together several heads turned, but there was no comment. French noticed it, without smiling. He gave the impression of being coiled, ready to lash out.

He was eating when suddenly he put his plate down. "We got twenty-two hundred head, Chantry. You want more?"

"No . . . let's move 'em out."

"Daybreak?"

"Yes."

"For Dodge?"

"No."

They all looked up then, surprised. French was the most surprised of all, Chantry thought, for until that time Chantry had left all the handling of the cattle to him.

"We'll take the longer route," Chantry said, "by way of Clifton House."

He realized he could not hope to compare his information about the area with that of French Williams, but they would not know how much or how little he knew, and must proceed accordingly.

"Have it your way," French said mildly. "There's more water, easier drives." He grinned at him. "And it will take longer."

Tom Chantry lay that night, looking up at the stars, and, tired as he was, there was little sleep in him. The way they would follow had been traveled by cattle herds occasionally, more often by pack trains, army commands, and mountain men, but every foot of it was alive with danger and trouble.

The men with whom he rode were silent toward

him. They did not trust his courage, and were not prepared to respect his leadership. Most important, perhaps, he had a partner in whom he must trust to some extent, but who had everything to gain by not getting the cattle through on time, or at all.

Lying there in the darkness, he felt suddenly very much alone, but he remembered something his father had said. "Don't ever be afraid of being alone, boy. The strongest man is he who stands alone."

And then Pa had added, "To just that extent that you lean on somebody, or rely on them, to that extent you are a weaker man."

Chapter 5

When the herd moved out in the morning Tom Chantry rode on ahead.

The stars were still in the sky, and the cattle were a bobbing mass of black without shape or substance. Then as the gray sky grew paler, here and there a horn glistened in reflected light, or a balky steer moved out from the herd and had to be shoved back.

Slowly a few of the cattle moved out ahead and the herd strung out along the trail, not an impressive sight to anyone who had seen buffalo in their great masses on this same grass, but this slim north-pointing finger was a symbol of change in the West.

The cattle could not exist here until the buffalo were gone, but in their time many of the cattle would go, too. Even as they displaced the buffalo, the forerunners of their own replacements were building shacks and stringing fences west of the Mississippi. Lone cabins appeared, with occasionally a barn, and a field plowed up.

Better than the others, Chantry knew what that meant, for he had lived in the East. The buffalo had to give way to cattle to feed the growing population of eastern cities; in their turn the cattle would go because farmers wanted to grow crops, they wanted to plant corn, wheat, and rye on the ground where the grazing grass grew.

Nor could the Indian, free-roving as he was, compete in his hunting and food-gathering existence with the farmer, for the Indians needed thousands of acres for even a small group to exist, and on much less ground the farmer could grow crops for himself and for shipment east.

Tom Chantry thought of the disappearing buffalo with regret, but he could not deny the inevitable.

French moved up beside him. "They're stringing out well, Chantry. We're off to an easy start." After a momentary pause he said, "Why'd you choose the long way? The Cut-Off is much the fastest. It's drier, but we could make it. Were you scared, or just cautious?"

"Maybe a little of both. Why take the chance?"

French glanced at him. "It doesn't seem to bother you much that the boys think you're yellow."

Chantry felt a quick surge of anger, but fought it down. His voice was calm when he replied. "It does bother me. There's still enough of the kid in me for it to bother a lot, but I've got enough man in me not to be a damn fool about it."

"You can't duck a showdown. You can only postpone it."

"Maybe. But when the showdown comes you'll be the first to know."

French looked at him sharply. "Are you saying that when you have a showdown it'll be with me?"

"That's hardly likely. I need you to get to Dodge. Anyway, I'm not a gunfighting man. Remember that."

"I'll be damned if I can figure you out, Chantry. You talk like a man with sand, but you sure don't act up to it."

"French, this will be a long drive. You know that better than I do. If I'm to get these cattle through I'd better stay alive, and I want you alive, too."

"What if it comes to gun trouble?"

"They tell me you're the fastest man in the country. I'll leave the gunfighting to you."

French Williams couldn't leave it alone. "But you can shoot? I mean, you're packing a Winchester . . . why?"

"Meat . . . we've men to feed, and I don't want to butcher my own cattle if I can help it."

"Can you hit anything?"

"Well," Chantry said seriously, "the man who sold me the rifle said that if I'd point it in the right direction I'd have a pretty good chance. Of course, he said, I'd have to hold steady. I'll give it a try sometime."

French was silent, uncertain whether Chantry was

serious or not. "What else did they tell you about me?" he asked finally.

"You know what they'd be likely to say. That your cows were the best in the country, giving you four or five calves a year . . . that sort of thing."

French grinned. "Maybe I'm just lucky," he said. He stood in his stirrups to scan the country ahead. "Why'd you pick me, then?"

"Because they said you might steal a man's cows, but you'd never cheat at cards. They said whatever else you were, you were a man of your word. Also, they said you had guts and knew cattle. I decided you were the man I wanted."

French swung his horse and rode back along the line of the drive.

Chantry, after a moment of hesitation, rode on ahead at a fast trot. He wanted to see the country, and if anybody was coming down the trail he wanted to see them first. He needed to know, needed desperately to know about that railroad.

He topped out on the low ridge that crossed the trail. Far off to the east he could see a moving black patch, some scattered black spots that must be buffalo. Nearer, there was nothing.

The sky was fantastically clear . . . no clouds, and a view that carried the eye away to a vast distance. The roan tugged at the bit, eager to be moving, but Chantry waited, studying the land. This was what he must do . . . he must learn to *see*, not merely to look. We must learn to recognize the things at which he looked, and to draw conclusions from them. Out here a man's life might depend upon it.

Despite his feelings about carrying a gun, he found himself occasionally wishing he had one. It was a kind of insurance.

Now, feeling alone upon the plains, facing the situation in which he had placed himself, he had time to be afraid. He could not help but think of what he was risking for himself and for Earnshaw, gambling that he could stay with the herd to its shipping point. The presence of Dutch Akin was a hint as to the lengths to which French Williams would go to drive him off.

Had French expected him to turn tail and run? It was more than likely. But he had not run, and now the next move was up to French.

Turning in his saddle, he looked back at the long line of cattle. He was more than a mile in advance of the drive and from where he sat he could see it to advantage. The men riding drag appeared only occasionally through the dust, but the flankers on either side he could see easily, and the two men riding point. Off to the east was the chuck wagon, and not far behind it the wranglers with the horse herd.

Twenty-two hundred head, give or take a few, and fifteen men to ride herd on them—sixteen, including himself. And ahead of them twenty to thirty days' drive, depending on conditions, and on how far west the railroad had progressed.

Aside from choosing the destination, he could do little in the way of planning. Their final destination was in his hands; the management of the herd and the men was up to French.

The season was well along. Here and there water holes would be drying up, but for most of the early part of the drive they would be near the Canadian or some of its branches.

To the east was buffalo country, and Indian country as well, and before very long they must turn east; at no time would they be safe either from Indians or from rustlers.

Chantry did not believe French would try to steal the herd . . . too many people knew the circumstances of their bargain, and French would deem it a personal failure to win by any means other than driving Chantry from the herd . . . or so Chantry believed.

For that reason, he must be wary of tricks. Searching back into his childhood, he tried to remember the tricks played by cowboys on trail drives or roundups. The bucking horse was the first and most obvious, and Chantry was sure that would come his way again. The rattlesnake in the blankets was another . . . or something that might appear to be a snake.

Worst of all, he had no friends in the crew, and Akin was the only one who even took the time to talk to him;

but that might change. Slowly, he studied them in his
mind, trying to pick out the ones who might at least
stand for fair play.

McKay . . . a short, stocky man with a shock of
rusty brown curls and a hard-boned face. He was
twenty-four or -five, a first-class bronc stomper and a
good hand with cattle. A steady man, asking no favors
of anyone, doing his share of the work and a little more.
He packed a gun, and by all accounts could use it.

Helvie . . . a quiet-mannered man, somewhat reserved, and four or five years older than McKay. A
good hand from Illinois, four years a soldier in the
frontier cavalry, a year as a freighter, and four years a
cowhand.

Hayden Gentry . . . called Hay Gent, from Uvalde,
down in Texas, his family among the first settlers west
of the Neuces. Long, lean, and tough as mule hide.
Easy-going, full of humor, and fast with a gun, so it
was said. Nobody wanted to be known as good with a
gun around French, not unless he was a trouble-hunter.

Rugger, Kincaid, and Koch were good hands, but
they were cronies of French, and probably not one of
them had been born with the name he was using. A
bad lot, as were most of the others.

Chantry rode on. The grass was dry, but there was
plenty of it. Twice he saw buffalo, but only a few, and
those were scattered out. Evidently they were on the
outer edges of the great herd, or were forerunners of
the herd.

The country was open, slightly rolling. Ahead
loomed Eagle Rock, near where they expected to bed
down for the night. Twice, Chantry drew up. He had
the eerie, uncomfortable feeling of being watched, but
he could see nothing, hear nothing. Nor was there any
movement within sight, only the brown grass on an occasional slope being bent by the wind.

There were no fresh tracks.

Suddenly wary, he swung his horse and rode off to
the west, scouting for sign. He found nothing. Tracks of
buffalo, occasionally old horse tracks. He stood in his
stirrups and looked off toward the breaks of the Canadian, not far to the east.

The creeks that flowed into the river had cut deep at places, and the sides were lined with heavy growth of trees and brush. In those breaks, Chantry reflected, an army could be hidden . . . it was something to consider.

He was high on a grassy hill with nothing in sight for a far distance when he heard the cry—a faint, choking cry, like nothing human, and it came from not far off. The roan, head up, ears pricked, looked off toward the right, toward the breaks of the Canadian.

Chantry waited, listening. Had it been human or animal? And if an animal, what kind could make such a sound? Suddenly he was sure the cry was human.

Turning his horse, he started in the direction the roan had looked, and peered ahead for the first glimpse of whatever it was.

He looked around slowly, studying the surroundings with infinite care. It might be a trap. He did not believe all he had heard of Indians, but he was cautious by nature. His horse walked forward, taking each step gingerly, as if ready to bolt. Obviously the roan did not like what it sensed was near.

Chantry's inclination was to turn and ride away, swiftly, for what lay before him was terror . . . perhaps horror. Instinctively he knew he should escape while it was still possible, but something urged him on . . . to see, *what?*

For a moment Chantry thought he could ride back, warn them of something ahead, and then approach this place with a dozen riders . . . yet what if there was nothing? He would have shown himself to be both a coward and a fool.

No, he knew he could not go back, and he rode on, walking his horse. He could feel its reluctance in the tenseness of its muscles, its urge to turn away.

Suddenly they topped the low rise and he was looking into a shallow place that sloped away with increasing steepness toward the river, but Chantry did not see that. All he saw was the man staked out before him. He dismounted and took a step nearer.

The man was stripped naked, hands and legs outspread, each ankle and each wrist tied to a stake. Al-

ready the sun had turned the white flesh a deep red in
ugly burns, but burns could be as nothing to him, for
he had been horribly mutilated.

In each thigh there was a deep gash along the top of
the muscle from the hip to the knee. His stomach had
been cut open and piled full of rock. The sides of his
face were cut, and the muscles of his biceps. For a frozen moment Tom Chantry stared, shocked motionless,
and then, of a sudden, his horse shied violently.

Turning sharply, he saw himself facing half a dozen
Indians. He saw them, saw their hands still bloody from
the deed before them, and realized his rifle was in its
scabbard on the saddle. It was no more than six feet
away, but it might have been as many miles. If he made
a move toward it, they could kill him. Would they?

Before him was the evidence. They had killed this
man. No doubt he had fought them, no doubt he was
an enemy taken in battle. As for himself, if he was to
survive he must face them down. He spoke suddenly,
keeping his tone moderate.

"This was not a good thing to do," he said, speaking
carefully. "One man could do you no harm."

One of the Indians spoke, surprisingly, in English.
"He do nothing to us. We find track. We follow. We
kill."

"Why?"

The Indian appeared to think the question foolish.
He replied simply, "Why not?"

"Go. I will bury him."

"All right." The Indian said something to the others
and they chuckled. "All right. You bury. Only him not
dead yet." Then admiringly, "He strong man. He no
cry, no beg. He laugh, he swear. Strong man."

What was he saying? The tortured man was not dead.

"I will bury him," he repeated. "You go."

"We watch," the Indian replied. Then he said, "You
strong like him?"

"Go," he said, fighting down the horror and the fear
that crept up within him. "Go." And surprisingly,
they went.

He stood for a moment, staring after them, not willing to accept what his eyes told him. Then from behind

him there was a shuddering groan. Chantry turned sharply.

The tortured man said, "If you got any water, I'd like it."

The tone was calm, controlled.

"You—you're *alive?*"

"It ain't for long. You git me that water and I'll be obliged."

Chantry turned swiftly to his horse and the canteen on the saddle horn. Kneeling beside the man, he held it to his lips. Feverishly, the man drank. For a moment he lay quiet and then he said, "I reckon that's the best thing I ever tasted."

"I'll untie you. I'll—"

"No! Don't you pay it no mind." The eyes opened and looked at him calmly. "I'm dead, man, can't you *see?*" And then he added, "I beat 'em! I beat those red devils at their own game! I never whimpered!

"You tell 'em that at the fort!" His voice was suddenly hoarse. "You tell 'em McGuinness never whimpered! Tell 'em that!"

"The chuck wagon is coming," Chantry said. "We have medicine, we—"

"Don't be a damn fool," the man said. "You tell 'em at the fort. You tell 'em—"

His voice faded away and his eyes suddenly were still. Chantry straightened to his feet. The man was dead . . .

Chapter 6

"Is he gone?"

Chantry faced sharply around. French Williams, Dutch Akin, Gent, Helvie, and Koch were on the rise behind him. All carried rifles.

"How could he be alive?"

"There wasn't much give in him," Hay Gent commented. "A man like that might live through anything."

"Ride to the wagon, Dutch," Williams said, "and bring up a shovel. We'll do the honors."

He glanced at Helvie. "You want to say the words? Or shall we let Chantry?"

"No!" Koch shouted. "I'll be damned if he will! Not over a man who died like that!"

Chantry felt himself go sick with shame, then fury. Suddenly he was in a killing rage. "Koch," he said, "I'll—"

"Shut up!" French laid his voice across them like a lash. "Helvie will read. Chantry, you'd better get back to the wagon while you're all together."

Chantry stood stiff, his anger vanished in the cold awareness that only Williams' intervention had saved him from another shooting situation.

"All right, but I hope you will notice that I was unarmed, yet the Indians did not attack me. If this man had done the same, perhaps—"

Helvie interrupted impatiently. "He was unarmed too. Can't you see? It didn't save him. If you'll look at the tracks . . . we followed them here. They raced beside him, striking, bedeviling him. Then they began the torture.

"This man was a soldier—a deserter perhaps. He had no gun. They killed his horse. Didn't you hear what the Indian said? The man had done nothing to them. He was a stranger, therefore an enemy. They were Kiowas.

It did not matter that this man was a white man. Had he been a Ute he would have fared no better."

"You *heard* them? You were *here?*"

"Why do you think they rode away? Because you were nice and peaceful. They left because they saw our guns on them from right over that ridge. We weren't begging a fight, and under the conditions neither were they."

French turned his back on him and walked away as Akin appeared with a shovel.

Tom Chantry hesitated, then swung into the saddle. He had made a fool of himself. Had not the others come when they did he might now be lying dead beside that dead man. Still, how could he *know?*

Nonetheless, he was displeased with himself. In their eyes he had come off badly. At best, he had been inadequate, and he did not like the feeling that he was despised. They were competent men who knew their jobs, men of proven courage and stamina, accepted by each other. He had proved nothing to anyone. Not even to himself. In their eyes he was a man who failed to measure up. They did not think him worthy to read the final words over a dead man.

It was hard to take, and he rode back to camp, ate, and turned in. Clifton House lay ahead, and there might be news. With luck the drive might be a short one.

Clifton House was a stage stop and a gathering place for cattle. Suddenly, before falling asleep, he made up his mind. He would ride on ahead, reach Clifton House well before the herd, and gather what information was available. Undoubtedly the herd would stop for the night not far from there, but he might learn whatever was known in time to change their route.

At daybreak he told Williams, "I'm riding to Clifton House. I'm expecting mail there."

"Better take somebody along to wipe your nose," Koch remarked. "There's some mighty mean men hang out at Clifton."

From one of the others he might have ignored it, but Koch was a sour, mean man with no breath of goodness in him, and after his remark of the day before Tom

Chantry was in no mood for any more of it. He put down his cup.

"Koch," he said, "I don't believe in killing men. I've no such feelings about giving one a whipping when he asks for it."

For a moment the camp was slack-jawed with amazement. Koch stared at him. "You gone crazy? Are you talkin' to *me?*"

"To you," Chantry got to his feet. "Just take off your gun belt."

Koch had the reputation of being a fist-fighter, and he liked to be known for it. He put down his plate and unbuckled his belt. "This here," he said, "is goin' to give me pleasure."

He got up, placing his gun belt on the ground, and he swung from that position. The blow was totally unexpected, and caught Chantry on the chin. His heels flew up and he hit the dust on the back of his shoulders, Koch rushing up to stamp on him. The cowpuncher's first kick was launched too soon and caught Chantry on the shoulder. It was the first time he had ever been kicked, and suddenly he realized that all he knew of fighting would do him no good unless he got into action fast.

Rolling over, he lunged to a crouching position and dived at Koch. The cowboy had been expecting Chantry to try to stand erect, and the sudden lunge made him step back quickly. On his high-heeled boots he staggered, and Chantry smashed into him.

Tom Chantry was lean and strong, and in good shape. He had boxed and wrestled a lot, but simply for fun. He had had only two fights since he was a man, both of them in the stockyards where he bought cattle, but the men with whom he had boxed and wrestled had been above average, and he knew how to handle himself.

Ugly with anger at being knocked into the dust, Koch was up quickly. He swung a looping right. Chantry saw it coming and stepped inside, smashing a right to the ribs that made the larger man gasp.

Koch grabbed him, tried to butt, then stamped on Chantry's instep with his boot heel. A stabbing pain went through Chantry's foot, and jerking back he threw the cowhand over his hip with a rolling hiplock.

Koch sprang to his feet and came in fast. He hit Chantry high on the cheek bone, splitting the skin. Another blow caught Chantry on the chin. Tom staggered, blocked a blow with his elbow, and countered with a stiff right to the body.

He was warmed up now, and suddenly he felt good. This was something he could do, and he liked to do it. Koch, at about one-ninety, was twenty pounds the heavier man, but he was slower. A skilled rough-and-tumble fighter, he knew nothing of boxing, and less of defense.

Tom Chantry had caught three brutally hard punches and was still on his feet. He had been down, but he had gotten up. He was sure Koch had hit him as hard as he was likely to, and he had taken the punches and was still coming.

He side-stepped as Koch swung, and hit the bigger man in the belly, but made no effort to follow it up. Koch wheeled, and came in slowly, looking for an opening. Tom feinted at the ribs, and when Koch dropped his hand, he hit him on the ear, splitting it and showering him with blood. When Koch's hands came up, Tom whipped an uppercut to the wind.

His timing was right now, Koch might be a good man with a gun and a brawler with some success, but Tom was realizing now that boxing was not in Koch's experience. He struck a stiff left to the face, and repeated it. He feinted another, then struck to the wind.

Koch moved in, and suddenly kicked for the groin. Chantry saw it just in time and, stepping back, tripped over an extended leg, whose leg he did not know. He staggered and fell, and Koch stamped at his head. Rolling away from Koch's boot heel, Chantry caught a vicious backward kick from Koch's Mexican spur, driven into the face.

Chantry lunged up from the ground. The viciousness of the attack appalled and infuriated him. He brushed a punch aside and smashed both hands to Koch's face in short, wicked hooks, and then as the man staggered back, Chantry broke his nose with an overhand right.

Blood was running down the side of his face, but Tom Chantry had no thought now but to destroy. He feinted, smashed another right to the already broken nose, then hooked both hands to the wind in short, lifting punches, and an overhand right to the side of the neck.

Koch staggered, and Chantry moved in, left and right to the face. Koch fell back against the chuck wagon and Tom uppercut to the wind, then smashed another right to the face. Koch started to fall, but Chantry caught him by the shirt and held him while he hit him in the face. Then he dropped him into the dust.

Chantry turned, looking at the men crowded around. "I don't believe in killing," he said, "but that doesn't mean I am yellow, or afraid to fight. If anybody has any argument they can step out now."

French had been sitting back, one leg crossed over the other. He uncrossed them now and stood up. "You'll leave us short-handed, Chantry, so you better leave it as it is."

He looked at the holes in Chantry's face made by the spur. "He drove it deep. You better have that looked at."

Chantry went to his horse and leaned his head into the saddle, his breath coming in great, tearing gasps. Slowly his breathing came back to normal and he began to feel the cuts and bruises. He took water from the barrel on the chuck wagon and bathed his face and his raw knuckles.

He had nothing with which to treat the deep cuts in his cheek, so he bathed it with whiskey. Then he returned to his horse, swung into the saddle, and rode away.

His knuckles were raw and bleeding. When out of sight of the herd he turned toward the Canadian, and at a small branch that flowed down to the river he dismounted to wash the blood from his hands. Suddenly he looked up and saw an Indian in a black hat standing on the other bank, watching him. His rifle was still in its scabbard, a dozen yards away. In his confusion after the fight and in his desire to bathe his knuckles, he had not remembered to keep the rifle with him. The Indian, had he wanted to, could have killed him by now.

Tom got slowly to his feet, and the Indian said, "Me Pawnee. Friend."

Chantry jerked his head to indicate the cattle, out of sight and some distance away. "I ride with the cattle."

"You have fight?"

"Yes," and with satisfaction he added, "I won."

The Pawnee sat down on a rock and took out the makings. When Chantry refused them, he began to build a cigarette. He gestured with the cigarette. "That is French Williams?"

"Yes."

"His herd?"

"Mine . . . if I get to the railroad on time. If I don't stay with him all the way, it becomes his."

The Pawnee looked at him. "He do this?"

"No. A man named Koch. I brought it on myself."

"Maybe." The Indian lit his cigarette. "Koch a bad man. I know."

Tom Chantry was trying to remember what he knew of the Pawnees. Great fighting men, among the best trackers, and they worked with white men as allies. He studied the Indian but his decision was already formed, and he liked what he saw.

"You gamble big," the Pawnee said, and added, "You do not go to Dodge?"

"Williams wanted to, but I've heard the railroad was coming on west. I did not tell him that and I do not believe he knows they have started building again. I think if we drive north, then east, we will meet it."

The Pawnee considered. "But they are his men? I think he will leave you. He will take his men. What you do with cattle then?"

"I'll drive the herd alone." He was talking nonsense, and knew it. "Or find some other riders."

He got to his feet. "Are you riding toward Clifton's?"

"Yes."

"Ride with me. Tell me about the country." And he added, "My father used to tell me the Pawnees were the bravest of warriors. He told me of the fight at Pawnee Rock."

"It was a fight."

"I am Tom Chantry."

"Sun Chief."

They rode for over an hour in silence, and when Clifton's was in sight Chantry said, "You want to work for me?"

"To herd cattle with French Williams? No."

"To scout for me." He drew up. "Find the railroad and tell me where it is. Check the water holes and tell me where there is water. I would not want you to come into camp at all. Report to me when you can, but where no one will see." He smiled. "Sun Chief, I want you to be my ace in the hole."

"All right. I do."

Tom Chantry reached in his pocket and withdrew a gold piece. "You ride for me and you will get another like this."

"I do. You keep. You pay all when finish." He pulled off. "I ride now."

Clifton House loomed ahead, and Tom Chantry trotted his horse toward it. The stage had just stopped and some people were getting down. One of them was a girl.

Chapter 7

Tom Chantry rode up to Clifton House and left his roan at the hitching rail. He glanced at the other horses . . . six saddled horses, and a buckboard. He had not yet acquired the westerners' habit of noting brands.

He went up the steps to the first-floor porch, and entered the door. Several men standing at the bar turned to glance at him, but none offered a greeting or comment. What his business was remained his business, no matter how curious they might be.

Chantry ordered a beer, then turned to the man beside him. "Join me?"

"Thanks."

He was a long-geared man in shotgun chaps and denim jacket, a faded blue shirt, and a tied-down gun. "It's a dry country," the man added.

"I'm heading north. Do you know the country along the Picketwire?"

"Some. I just come over it."

"Water up there?"

"Enough. But no more than enough. The range is dryin' up." He lifted the beer. "*Salud.*"

"Cheers." Chantry drank, then said, "I'm Tom Chantry. Driving north with a trail herd."

"Bone McCarthy. I'm driftin'."

They talked in a desultory fashion, but with half his attention Chantry was listening for mention of the railroad.

"Seems a shame," McCarthy was saying.

"What?"

"Them Injuns. Takin' the country off 'em. In good times it must've been a fine life they had, huntin' and fishin', or driftin' down the country on the trail of the buffalo. I ain't sure what we'll do to the country will be any better."

"Have you lived among them?"

"Brought up around 'em. I've fought 'em off an' on since I was a kid, and they're good fighters. Maybe the best."

"But we've whipped them. The army has, I mean."

"Lucked out, I'd say. Mighty few Injuns have rifles, and never enough ammunition to last out a fight, but you never seen their like for creepin', crawlin', bein' where they ain't expected.

"It won't be at war that the white man whips 'em. He'll beat them with his store-bought things. When the Injun made all he needed he had no troubles to speak of, but the white man showed him all sorts of things he was greedy for, and now he wants 'em. He has to get 'em by war or by trade."

"Whiskey?"

"That's the least of it, believe me. Knives, guns, pots, pans, and such. The Indian was whipped the first time a white trader came amongst them to trade with things the Injun couldn't make with his own hands."

"I hadn't looked at it that way."

Bone McCarthy took a swallow of his beer. "You're ridin' with a herd? Whose?"

"Mine . . . if I can stay with it to the railhead. French Williams is trail boss."

"Williams? You got you a live one, *amigo*. He's hell on wheels with a gun."

"Do you know him?"

"Can't say I do, but there's talk goes up the trail. What did you mean when you said it was your herd if you stayed with it?"

Chantry explained, and to leave nothing out he coolly told why he was forced to make such a deal, and also spoke of his feelings about guns.

McCarthy listened in silence. It was obvious that the others at the bar, or some of them, heard what Chantry was saying. He did not care. He had acted as he saw fit.

"You're carryin' some bruises. Did you get throwed?"

"No. Because I wasn't anxious to shoot, a man

named Koch questioned my courage. We had a bit of a go-around. I whipped him."

He drank his beer. The conversation along the bar began again, and Chantry asked McCarthy, "Did you ever run across a Pawnee named Sun Chief?"

"Uh-huh. Good man. He was one of Major North's Pawnee scouts. Got wounded and had to drop out. Heard he was up and around again."

"I hired him to scout the trail for me, the trail to the railhead."

"You takin' on anybody else? I'm rustlin' work."

Tom Chantry drained his glass. "McCarthy, you heard my story. I'm not a man who believes in guns, and there are some who think I'm yellow. You still want to join me?"

McCarthy shrugged. "Every man's entitled to think the way he chooses, the way I see it. I think you're wrong, and I think the time'll come when you'll pay for it. What you're sayin' is that I got to take my own chances that you'd back me up in a tight spot, ain't that it?"

Chantry felt anger stir within him, and with it a feeling of resentment. Why could things never be simple? Yet, what would he do if it came to that? Supposing he was caught in a situation where he must fight or die? Or worse still, where he must fight or one of his men would die?

"You'd have to gamble on it, McCarthy," he said. "I believe a lot more can be done by reason than by guns."

"All right. You trust to reason," McCarthy said, "but you won't mind if I wear my guns, will you?"

"As you like. I'm not a reformer."

McCarthy lifted his beer. "Luck," he said. "You're sure a-goin' to need it."

He ordered another beer. "This'll have to be the last," he said. "I ain't carryin' any more money." When the beer arrived he said, "Now that I'm workin' for you, what do I do?"

"Bring your beer along," Chantry suggested, "and we'll sit over there at the table. I'm going to order us a couple of dinners and you're going to tell me every way you can think of that Williams might use to drive me off the herd."

For an hour they talked. Bone McCarthy was a cool, knowledgeable man with much experience on cattle drives and roundups. He ran through the possible ruses, one by one. Bad horses, Indian scares, maybe a rattlesnake in the bed. "He may even have put Koch up to jumpin' you. It's the sort of thing he might do."

After a while McCarthy was silent, but he seemed to have something on his mind that he hesitated to say.

"What is it?" Chantry asked.

Bone looked up at him, then filled both their coffee cups. "You know damn well what he'll do, Chantry. He'll have somebody brace you with a gun. He'll catch you when you're armed, and you'll have no excuse."

"I simply won't shoot."

Bone stared at him. "You don't seem to read the sign," he said. "If you don't shoot, he'll kill you . . . whoever French Williams gets to bully you into a fight. It won't matter one damn what you do, whether you drop your gun or whatever, he'll shoot, and shoot to kill."

"He'd kill me for that herd?"

"You must be dreamin', man. Of course he will. He'd kill his whole outfit for that herd. Right now I'd say the odds are a hundred to one against you makin' the next fifty miles."

They stopped talking then, but Tom Chantry considered the matter. French Williams was a known thief. He had killed men. He might offer an appearance of fair play for the look of the thing, but Bone was sure to be right. Somebody who rode with them would challenge him, and at his first move, would shoot and shoot to kill . . . any move Chantry made would be construed as a move for a gun—a move to shoot.

The only thing he could do was avoid carrying any weapon at all. He said as much.

McCarthy shrugged. "Worse comes to worst, they'll get you out on the grass somewheres, shoot you, and plant a gun on you. It's been done."

He looked hard at Chantry. "Can you shoot? I mean, did you ever use a gun?"

"I can shoot. I've hunted a lot."

"How about with a hand gun?"

"Yes. I've used one."

"Can you draw? I mean, can you get a gun out of your holster without dropping it?"

"Yes. My father showed me when I was a youngster. He had me practice. But I never liked it."

"Just get it out, and no matter what he does, even if you get hit, you level that gun and shoot. Take your time, but make that first shot count. You may never get another one."

"There's no use to talk of it. I won't be carrying a gun."

"Well, in case you change your mind, you make that first one do the job. I've seen many a fast-draw artist who got his gun out quicker'n scat, an' then put his first bullet right out in the dust betwixt 'em, an' never got another shot."

Chantry pushed back from the table. "Here's what I want you to do." He put a twenty-dollar gold piece on the table. "Get yourself some grub, and then you keep an eye on the herd. You see whatever goes on, but you keep out of sight. If anything happens that you think I ought to know, you get in touch with me. I'll be riding out from the herd every day."

"All right." Bone McCarthy stood up.

"You watch yourself, do you hear?"

The tawny plains swept away in all directions, a gently rolling stretch of grama and buffalo grass with patches of greasewood; over some of the higher levels the plain was dotted with Spanish bayonet, or yucca. Far off, the moving black mass of a small herd of buffalo showed against a brown slope, and in a gully the stark white of scattered bones.

The herd was behind him again and he rode warily, without his rifle, carrying only the bowie knife he carried for work around the camp, or casual use. His eyes swept the horizon, hesitating here and there . . . but nothing moved.

The dust held no tracks, and when he came up to the river bed he saw that it was dry and cracked into plate-sized slabs of gray mud, baked and crisp.

No water.

Chantry mopped the sweat from his face and squinted his eyes against the sun. It was mid-afternoon, and the herd had been without water since daybreak . . . there had been an expectation of water at this place.

French Williams had mentioned casually, in an off-hand manner that they would water here. Had he known the creek was dry? Chantry suspected it, but had no way of knowing.

It was twenty miles to the next water, which meant a dry camp tonight, with a parched and restless herd, hard to hold. He glanced at the sun. Had they swung farther west? Williams was pointing the herd now. This morning it had been Koch.

Williams knew far more about the ways of cattle on a drive than Chantry would ever know, and he had driven over this country before . . . whether by this route or not, Chantry did not know. Undoubtedly the man had a plan of operation, and was not proceeding in a haphazard manner. He was a cool head, seemingly reckless and careless, but Chantry had quickly divined that the gunman was basically cautious.

He scanned the horizon again. Here at the river bank there was a little brush, and further away there were trees. Turning his horse down the dry watercourse, he walked it slowly toward the trees. There might be water down there, some isolated pool where he could at least water his horse.

Even while his senses were alert to the surroundings, he was considering his problem. He now had two assets in Sun Chief and Bone McCarthy, neither of them known to French Williams. But his greatest asset was the fact that French Williams underrated him, considered him a tenderfoot. He on his part was aware that Williams was a dangerous and treacherous adversary. That is, he knew from his own guesses and from what McCarthy had said, and it was enough to make him cautious.

Tall cottonwoods suddenly loomed ahead and the

watercourse was so narrow that he could no longer proceed. Ahead of him it narrowed into a rocky channel, impassable for a horse, and fell off sharply into a canyon.

He rode up the bank and into the trees. There, in their dappling shade, he paused to listen.

The cottonwoods rustled, somewhere a crow cawed into the hot afternoon, and then he heard a low murmur, followed by a faint clink, as of metal on metal.

Dismounting, he tied his horse with a slipknot, and walked cautiously forward, moving from tree to tree. Back in the East he had often stalked game in the woods, and he knew how to move quietly.

Suddenly the ground dropped away before him and he was looking into a small, grassy park scattered with cottonwoods, with willows growing along the streambed. Near the edge of the willows two men sprawled lazily near a dying fire. They were too far off to identify them, but he had no need, for their horses were grazing nearby, and one of them was the horse he had ridden out of Las Vegas.

The Talrim boys! Hank and Bud Talrim, who had taken his horse at gun point.

He drew back, and carefully made his way to his horse. Mounting, he rode back the way he had come.

What were the Talrim boys doing *here?*

Of course, they might have gone anywhere. But they were escaping from the law, and one would imagine they would keep on running. Instead, they had for some reason circled back and were now here, close by his herd.

Curious, he rode back to the herd, switched his saddle to his other horse, and rode out again. Glancing back, he saw Williams staring after him, but he rode ahead directly east from the herd, cutting for sign. He had gone only three miles when he found it—the tracks of two riders, tracks not many hours old, and one set was the tracks of his own horse.

All right. So they had come up from the south, but that was necessary, for when he had met them they were heading south. He back-tracked them for several miles on a route parallel to the herd. On at least one occasion they had ridden high enough on a low hill to look over and watch the herd.

In itself, that meant nothing. They could have heard the lowing of the cattle and simply come to take a look. On the other hand, it was worth thinking about. Was it simply coincidence?

He had to remember that French Williams had gone to the trouble of locating and hiring Dutch Akin. Had he somehow gotten in touch with the Talrim boys? Were they to be his ace in the hole?

They were known murderers . . . wanted men. Would they kill for hire? They would. They would even kill simply to kill.

He swung his horse from their trail and started back to the drive.

For the first time he found himself wanting a gun. He was a fool, he told himself. With such men as the Talrims one did not reason. One did not sit down and discuss their mutual problems, because there were none. These men were killers.

This was a different land from the East, ruled by a different set of principles. The circumstances and conditions were different; it was a land to which law had not yet come, nor the restraints that society can exercise upon its members.

Heretofore he had been protected, one man of many who were protected by law, by the pressures of society, by fear of retribution. He had not had to fear, for other men stood between him and danger, but here there were no such men. A man was expected to stand on his own feet, to protect himself.

He was realizing how cheap are the principles for which we do not have to fight, how easy it is to establish codes when all the while our freedom to talk had been fought for and bled for by others.

Tom Chantry was no fool. He had won his battle with Dutch Akin by restraint and reason, but he was wise enough to know that neither of these would prevail against such men as the Talrim boys. Reason or restraint would seem weakness to them, and they were the kind to strike quickly when they discovered weakness. They had been quick to take his horse when they discovered he did not carry a gun, and they had shot at him, almost casually, as an afterthought, not caring greatly whether they killed or not.

He looked off in the direction in which his cattle had gone, then touched his spur lightly to his horse's ribs. He would go back. It was time. There were decisions to be made.

Chapter 8

The cattle moved north with the rising of the sun, stirring the dust across the short-grass prairies, blue grama with occasional patches of little bluestem and curly-leaved sedge, and on some slopes a scattering of prickly pear. The cattle moved slowly, grazing as they walked, and Tom Chantry rode the drag, considering his problem.

Dutch Akin switched horses and rode back to join him, lifting a hand as he passed, hitching his bandana over his nose to keep out the dust.

It was very hot. McKay went by, circling to bring a bunch-quitter back to the drive. When he had driven the steer where he belonged he dropped back, riding beside Chantry.

They had fallen back to be clear of some of the dust and to keep an eye on any laggards that might cut out for the flanks.

"Quite a whippin' you gave Koch," McKay commented, "an' he had it comin'."

"There's a difference," Chantry said, "between a man who doesn't want to kill anybody and a man who's afraid. He just wasn't reading the sign right."

"You be careful," McKay said. "He's been talkin' that it ain't over."

At the nooning Chantry rode in to switch horses, and got his saddle on the little buckskin that was one of the horses allotted for him to ride. He planned to scout wide of the herd that day, as he went to the wagon for his rifle.

As he stepped up to the wagon he heard Koch grumbling about something nearby, then heard his voice suddenly grow quiet. He read nothing into it, but had just drawn his rifle clear of the wagon when Koch said,

"All right, you blasted tenderfoot! Now you got a gun, turn an' start shootin'."

The rifle barrel was in Tom's left hand, which gripped it close to the fore-sight. Koch was not more than a dozen feet from him, and Tom wheeled sharply, swinging the rifle. As he came around he let it go, sending it flying toward the big man's face.

Koch ducked and Tom Chantry lunged at him. The big man staggered, caught his balance and swung the gun around, but it went off of itself before he brought it into line. With the smashing report the cattle suddenly lunged and were running.

Chantry hit Koch with his shoulder, knocked him sprawling, then fell on him, knees in the big man's belly. Without moving a knee, Chantry swung two hard punches at his face. Then he leaped back and, as Koch started to rise, smashed him in the face with his knee.

Men had leaped to the saddle and were plunging after the stampeding cattle, which were frightened by the sudden shot.

Chantry waited a moment for Koch to get up, but thoroughly angry now, he walked up to him and struck him twice in the face before Koch could lift his hands, hit him in the belly, and then when he started to fall forward, brought a hammer blow down on his kidneys.

"You're fired, Koch," he said. "Get your outfit and get out. I don't ever want to see you around again . . . anywhere." Chantry picked up his rifle and walked to his horse.

He rode out, swept wide, and began gathering cattle, pushing them toward the center. He gathered about twenty head, and then came upon a bunch that had slowed to a walk, and started them all back. Hay Gent joined him with a dozen head.

"What happened back there?" Gent asked.

"With Koch? I whipped him again, and then I fired him."

"What if he won't stay fired?"

"He will."

"But if he don't?"

"Then I'll whip him again, and again, until he stays fired."

Gent made no comment, and they drove the cattle in, meeting McKay, Helvie, and Rugger also bringing in cattle. It was the work of hours, but slowly the cattle were all gathered.

"We'll move on," French said. "Maybe there's water up ahead." He looked around. "Where's Koch?"

They were all listening. "I fired him," Chantry replied. "That shot started the stampede. This is no place to be settling personal grudges."

Williams looked at him thoughtfully. "We'll be short-handed," he said. And he added, "He'll carry a grudge. Likely he'll lay for you."

"He'll have company then," Chantry said.

"What's that mean?" Williams asked quickly.

"Men leave tracks, French. I'm not so much a tenderfoot that I can't read sign."

They were all looking at him, but he left it at that, and the cattle started to move.

Riding out from the herd, he found a promontory and rode cautiously up the side to look over the ridge and survey the country. A few miles ahead and off to the right of the trail there was a hollow with a touch of deeper green.

Half an hour later he came up to it, a wide slough boggy along the sides, but with water a-plenty. Skirting it, he found it had a gravelly shore, and turned back to guide the herd.

"Water?" French was skeptical. "I don't know of any water around here."

"You do now," Chantry said. "Hay, turn the herd."

Hay Gent glanced at Williams, who merely shrugged, so the herd swung. By the time the cattle had watered and a few head had been snaked out of the mud it was coming on to sundown, and over by the chuck wagon there was a fire going.

There was little talk around the fire. The men were dog-tired, and when they had eaten they hunted their bedrolls. French alone loitered at the fire, smoking. From time to time he glanced across at Tom Chantry.

"You are a difficult man, my friend," he said at last. "Whatever else you may be, you are not a coward."

"Thanks."

"I will win, however. It's a long way to Dodge."

"It is that." Chantry looked up from his coffee. "And when you get there, I'll be with you."

French's gaze hardened, then he laughed. "You might be at that," he replied cheerfully, "and if you are, I'll give you credit for it."

"You'll need the credit," Chantry replied. "I'll have the cash."

He got a plate and his food, and sat down a bit away from the fire. If they didn't accept him, the hell with them—he could go his own way. But there was something in him that was different now; he had grown harder, tougher. The wide plains and the long winds of morning were having their effect; but French Williams the Talrim boys, and Koch had contributed . . . yes, and Sparrow back there at Las Vegas, and Bone McCarthy at Clifton's. These men had experienced far more living in the West than he had. Perhaps, he thought reluctantly, perhaps his thinking needed a bit of revision.

How much of what he believed about not using guns was left over from that bitter day when they brought his father home on a shutter? Or was it what his mother had taught him? Deep in grief over the death of his father, she had shrunk from the possibility of such an end for her son.

Killing was wrong—on that score he could not change. However, there was no law here except the law enforced by men with guns, and did such men as the Talrims, and even such men as Williams himself, understand any other law?

If a man would not put restrictions upon himself, if he would not conform to the necessary limits that allow people to live together in peace, then he must not be allowed to infringe on the liberties of those who wanted to live in peace. And that might lead to violence, even to killing.

The trouble was that back east men had lived so long in a society that demanded order and conformity that they failed to understand that there were societies where violence was the rule, and where there were men to whom only the fear of retribution placed a bridle on their license.

But Tom Chantry knew there was more than his father behind him, for the fighting tradition of the Chantrys did not begin with him, nor with his grandfather, who had stood with LaFitte and Jackson at the battle of New Orleans. There were generations before that, who had crossed over from Ireland.

The principal thing he had learned was that simply because he himself did not believe in violence was no reason that others would feel the same. In the future he must be more wary. But what if the Talrim boys' presence was not coincidence? What if French *had* arranged for them to be near? What if French intended the Talrim boys to eliminate him?

At daybreak he was out riding the drag, and when he broke off he caught up another horse from the remuda. This was a *grulla* mustang, small but wiry.

"Watch him, *amigo*," Dutch Akin whispered. "That one is mean."

The little mouse-colored horse stood quiet until saddled, but just as Chantry put his foot in the stirrup and rested his weight on it to swing to the saddle, the little horse folded up like a closing knife and then snapped open viciously. Tom Chantry slapped into the saddle as the horse came down, was almost thrown as it sunfished wickedly, then crow-hopped for half a dozen jumps, and switched ends suddenly. More by luck than anything else, Tom stayed in the saddle. He had ridden spirited horses, but nothing that bucked like this. Just as he was sure he was going to have to grab for the pommel with both hands, the *grulla* stopped bucking, ran a few steps, and settled down.

Chantry rode over to the chuck wagon and, taking his rifle, shoved it into the saddle scabbard. Then he turned and rode out on the plains.

He had not ridden more than half a mile when he saw a rider emerge from a draw just ahead and stand waiting. It was Bone McCarthy.

"Howdy, boss. You huntin' comp'ny?"

"Why not?"

"I ain't been up to you sooner because I figured you knew about them. I mean I saw your tracks back yonder."

"The Talrims? Yes, I saw them."

"I can't decide what they're after. They're traveling too slow unless they've got somethin' on their minds. Whatever it is concerns you or that herd. Every now and then they crest a ridge to study you."

Chantry had his own ideas about the reason for their presence. Somehow, he felt, French Williams had gotten word to them, and they were lying in wait for their chance to kill him. He might be mistaken, but there was the presence of Dutch Akin as an indication that Williams thought along such lines.

"They've dogged your trail a couple of times. I'd ride careful, if I was you."

"Any sign of Sun Chief?"

"Not hide nor hair." McCarthy dug into his saddlebag for a strip of jerky and began chewing on it. "Chantry, you're ahead of your time in this country— I mean, you not wantin' to carry a gun. This ain't the kind of world you came from, and it won't be for a few years. Whenever a man enters a new country like this his way of livin' drops back hundreds of years. You ain't livin' in the nineteenth century here, Chantry."

"You don't talk much like a cowhand."

"That's nonsense. Whoever said a cowhand was any special breed? Cowhands, like freighters, bankers, and newspaper editors, are apt to come from anywhere. They just like the life . . as I do."

Chantry glanced at him. "Where did you come from, McCarthy?"

"Ireland . . . where else? Twelve years ago I left there, but at the end of the War Between the States I went back for a few weeks, and got into trouble again."

"Again?"

"The first time I was visiting a friend in Glenveagh and there was trouble over an eviction . . . I had to leave the country. I joined up with the French, as many a good Irish lad has done over the years, and after a bit I migrated to this country. I had two years in the war, then back there, and straight away I got into the Fenian troubles and was lucky to get out with a whole skin. Back here again, and two years fightin' Indians with the Fifth Cavalry."

"The McCarthys are an old family, I've heard."

"Yes, some say we're the oldest family in Ireland. We owned Blarney Castle at one time."

"How does it happen that sometimes you talk as if you'd been born in the West."

McCarthy shrugged. "Saves questions. A good many men do it, you'll find. They just fall into the habit as I have, of talkin' the western way. You put on a way of talkin' when you change your clothes. It's as simple as that."

They rode on, scouting the country. "By the way," Bone McCarthy said, "back there at Clifton's the day I met you there was a girl there."

"I saw her."

"Well, she saw you. And she's been askin' questions. Aside from the fact that you're a handsome, upstanding man, why would she be so all-fired curious?"

"I don't know. She was a pretty girl, I remember that."

"I remember it too, but I've got an idea neither of us should. I've got a nose for trouble."

"She was asking questions?"

"She was. She was askin' the wrong questions, too. I mean, not questions a girl would ask who was interested in a man . . . but questions of somebody who wanted to know where you was goin', what route you'd be likely to take, and how many hands you had workin' for you."

"It doesn't make sense," Chantry commented.

"It did to her," McCarthy said dryly.

Chapter 9

The girl did not concern him. She would not be the first curious person he had encountered, and women had a way of asking questions about strange young men who are, or seem to be, unattached . . . and vice versa. Tom Chantry was more concerned with the Talrims and with worrying over when Sun Chief would reappear.

The cattle had moved slowly. Water holes were scarce, and it seemed they came to them early in the afternoon when French Williams invariably suggested it would be risky to drive on and make a dry camp. Twice at least his claims had undoubtedly been correct, for they were followed by long, dry drives.

On the drive itself all went well. The cattle were well broken to the trail, there was no friction among the riders, and nobody was troubling Chantry. His two victories over Koch seemed to have settled the matter of how much nerve he had, and the stampede caused by Koch had meant much additional work for them; they wanted no repeat performance.

Hard though the work might be, it had settled into routine, and this, Tom Chantry knew, increased his danger. Routine had a lulling effect upon the senses, and he knew his security demanded that he be alert at any moment for whatever might come.

Despite his impatience, he had to recognize that the short drives were having their effect on the cattle. Settled down after their stampede, the short days offered more time for grazing and they had gained weight. If nothing happened to change their present rate of progress and if the grazing continued to be good, the herd would arrive at market in excellent condition.

Was this what Williams was thinking of? Or was it something else? Why was he moving so slowly? Was he, too, waiting for word from the railroad?

There was no sign of Sun Chief.

Bone McCarthy was close by, and several times, riding out from the herd, Chantry came upon his tracks, as well as those of the Talrims, who seemed to have been joined by a third person. The new set of tracks were those of a smaller, shod horse.

Trinidad was not far ahead, and although it was only a small settlement it had already acquired a reputation as a tough place. In 1859 Gabriel Gutierrez and his nephew had come up from New Mexico with a herd of sheep. The men built a cabin on the south bank of the river and settled down there, grazing their sheep, hunting and farming a few acres of land. Others moved in, and the settlement was named for the daughter of Trinidad Baca, one of the first-comers.

Was French Williams waiting for something to happen at Trinidad? Chantry told himself he was imagining things.

"I got to hand it to you," Williams said one night as they sat by the fire. "You've done your share. You've stood up to the work better than I figured you would. You've changed, too. These last days you've honed down and sharpened up considerably."

"Thanks. You've done your job, too."

Williams chuckled. "But we still haven't reached Dodge and the railroad."

"Call it off if you want to," Chantry replied carelessly. "I'll pay you the going price for your herd on delivery at Dodge."

"You quitting on me? Trying to welch on your deal?"

"You know better than that. Just trying to let you make a dollar. Don't worry, French. When we deliver these cattle, I'll be there to collect."

"You got any idea what's ahead?" Williams studied him, his amusement apparent. "The Kiowas are out, and believe me, nobody is worse. They'll give us bloody hell."

"And there's been no rain, so we'll have water trouble. And there are rustlers. You've told me all that." Chantry leveled his eyes at Williams. "And don't pull another Dutch Akin on me. I won't stand for it."

"What will you do?"

Chantry knew the hands around the fire were listening, but he did not care. "If anybody shows up hunting me, French, I'll figure he was sent by you."

"And then?" Williams' voice was low.

"I'll take your gun away and break your neck."

Williams laughed. "I'd kill you, Chantry. Nobody will ever put hands on me the way you did with Koch. Gun or no gun, I'd kill you."

"Better have your gun out when you see me coming, then. You'll never get a chance to draw it." He got to his feet and walked over to the chuck wagon for the coffeepot. Coolly, he filled Williams' cup and then his own, putting the pot down by the fire. "And while you're at it, French, you'd better tell those Talrim boys to light a shuck. They might lead to some misunderstanding."

He looked at French, and suddenly he smiled. "I wouldn't want to break your back and then find it was all a mistake. You tell them to light out, will you?"

French Williams shook his head. "Chantry, if I wasn't so set on beating you out of that herd, I could like you."

The next day broke cold and raw, with a long wind in their faces, and the cattle had to be forced into it. And the wind did not let up as the sun rose behind the low gray clouds.

There would be water in the Picketwire where they would camp, and some shelter in the river bottom, if they were lucky. Tom Chantry rode the drag for a while, spelling a rider there, then he moved up into a swing position. After the noon break he took the *grulla* from the remuda and went scouting.

It was still cold, and he wore a buckskin jacket over his blue wool shirt. He went directly east, riding warily. Twice he came upon pony tracks; each time they were several days old. He held to low ground, climbing the ridges only to peer over the crest, showing himself as little as possible. He was uneasy, and after a bit he took his rifle from its scabbard and held it in his hand.

The wind was raw. He turned up the collar of his jacket, tucked his chin into it, and pulled his hat low.

He was studying the ground, then suddenly looked up to see he had ridden right into the bend of an elbow of hills. He must either skyline himself by crossing the ridge or follow along the side until he could reach the cattle trail. It was the country ahead he wanted to see, but caution told him the longer way was best.

He had turned to ride along the side of the hill when he glimpsed a notch, almost at the bend of the elbow, a small gap by which he could get to the other side of the ridge without showing himself on top of it. He swung his horse toward the notch.

His horse scrambled up the last few feet. At the opening of the notch he could see only that it was a sort of cleft in the ridge that seemed to lead all the way through. Old tracks told him the buffalo used this route, so it must go all the way through.

He walked his horse into the gap, traveled about a hundred yards, then suddenly rounded a low shoulder of the hill and emerged on the other side.

He never heard the shot, but he felt the blow. It was as if somebody had struck him suddenly across the side of the head with a whipstock.

He knew he was hit, he felt himself falling, he remembered the necessity of clinging to his rifle. He hit the dirt, smelled the dust that rose, and then he neither felt nor heard anything but the vague sound of his horse

Cold . . . icy, teeth-chattering cold. It was cold that brought him to consciousness, it was cold that opened his eyes.

It was night . . . cold and black, and there was a smell of rain in the air, and a distant rumble of thunder. He was lying sprawled on the earth, the smell of dust and parched grass in his nostrils. He started to move, a spasm of pain went through him. He lay still, wanting no more of that.

He had been shot. He had fallen from his horse. He had been shot sometime in the middle of the afternoon, but if anybody was looking for him they could scarcely fine him here.

A spatter of rain struck his shoulders. Shelter . . . he must find shelter. He risked the pain, and tried to sit up. On the third attempt he made it.

He was still at the cleft of the hills where he had been shot. He felt around him for his rifle . . . it was gone.

His knife? Gone. He felt then for his money, but it was gone, too. It was only then that he realized how cold his feet were.

His boots were gone.

Gingerly, he touched his head, which throbbed with a dull, heavy beat. His hair was matted with blood. He got to his knees, then shakily to his feet. He looked around slowly, blinking against the pain.

His horse was gone, too. He remembered then that he had heard it running off. It might not have gone far, and he called out. There was no sound in answer, no sound and no movement but the falling rain.

He staggered to the lip of the cut and looked around, but it was too dark to see anything.

The herd would be ahead and to his left. Taking a careful step at a time, he moved slantingly down the hill, toward the northwest. He stumbled over a rock and fell. When he got heavily to his feet, he realized that the butts of his palms were bloody, skinned in the fall.

Whoever had shot him, had left him for dead—or if not dead, sure to be dead soon.

He fell three times before he reached the bottom of the slope, and by then his socks were worn through and his feet were hurting. He peered about, trying in the distant flashes of lightning to see something he might use for shelter, but there was nothing.

First of all, rain or no rain, he needed some protection for his feet. Fumbling in the debris at the foot of the rocky slope, he found a jagged piece of rock, and removing his buckskin jacket he sawed off the sleeves a little above the elbows. He slipped these over his feet and used thongs made from the long fringes, knotted together, to tie the sleeves around his ankles.

Putting on his coat again, he moved out, walking carefully, trying to avoid the rocks and the patches of prickly pear.

A dark line ahead warned him of trees, and he went even more slowly, wary of Indians who might be camped there. Under the cottonwoods he stood close to a tree trunk and listened to the falling rain and the rustle of water in the creek bed, but he could hear no other sounds.

His eyes searched for a fire, or some evidence of human life, but there was nothing. He worked his way among the trees until he found a place where several bigger ones were grouped together in such a way that their entwined branches made a sort of shelter.

Here he leaned against a tree trunk and closed his eyes with weariness. After a moment he opened them, and his eyes, now accustomed to the darkness, saw a fallen limb from one of the cottonwoods. He went to it and, huddling there in its partial shelter, he leaned back against the tree, and slept.

Around him the rain fell softly, steadily. Overhead the cottonwoods rustled. In the hollow of a tree not twenty yards away a squirrel peered out at the rain for a moment, listening, then tucked its bushy tail around it once more and went back to sleep. . . . In a saloon in Trinidad a cowhand on the drift lighted a cigar and glanced at his cards. "I'll take two cards," he said.

More than a thousand miles to the east a girl in a white dress with lace at the throat looked down the table at her father and said, "Pa, I haven't heard from Tom. It isn't like him."

Earnshaw looked up, and said quietly, "I hope everythink is all right with him. I have written to him, telling him what has happened here. Everything depends on him now."

She was a gentle-appearing and lovely girl, but in the coolness of her eyes now and the set of her chin there was something that reminded her father that she came of pioneer stock. "Pa, I want to go west," she said. "I want to go to him."

"That's impossible. He's out on the range. From what I hear it's very wild country."

"He may need help."

"What help do you think you could give? You are a single girl, and we have no friends there, no one to whom you could go. It would be unseemly."

"Nevertheless, I want to go."

"Wait. We will hear from him."

Chantry awoke, shaking with a chill. He was wet through to the skin, without shelter, without food, without fire. He had lost blood, and he was very weak. He had no shoes, only the crude moccasins made from his sleeves.

He struggled to his feet and clung for a moment to the trunk of the cottonwood. He was shaky and uncertain, but he knew he must move, he must get on. A faint light under the trees indicated that daylight was not far off. He picked up a broken branch from the ground. It was almost straight, and was about seven feet long and almost two inches in diameter. Using it for a staff, he started to walk. For the first time he realized how sore his feet had become, but step by step he went through the cottonwoods to the far side.

By now the herd would be moving, or about to move. To overtake it in his present condition would be impossible. He had left the herd by riding east, and at a rough guess he must be about fifteen miles from Trinidad.

The clouds were low, the light still dim, and there were no landmarks visible. Fisher's Peak or the Spanish Peaks would have given him direction, but they were out of sight behind the clouds. Yet there was something he could go by.

Leaning on his staff in the partial shelter of a tree, he furrowed his brow against the throbbing in his skull, and thought of the Purgatoire, called by cattlemen the Picket wire. It lay ahead of him, crossing his line of travel had he been with the herd. The creeks in this area flowed north into the Picketwire, so the nearby creek would be flowing north, or in that general direction. To reach Trinidad he must turn at right angles to the flow of the creek and keep it at his back, and so go west.

Nobody would be looking for him. Williams had everything to gain and nothing to lose if Chantry never turned up again, or if he failed to be riding with the herd when it reached the railhead.

His body was chilled through, but he started on weaving a slow way among the trees. He managed a dozen steps before he stopped, then another ten. Ahead of him he could see the bank that marked the edge of the river bottom; once he climbed that bank he would be in the open, without any shelter at all.

Yet he could be no wetter than he now was, and not much colder. His only hope lay in keeping moving. Ten steps . . . then five. The buckskin on his feet would not last long. There was one thing to be thankful for: no Indian was fool enough to be out in the rain.

He came to the small bluff that marked the river bottom, and blinking his eyes in the rain, he looked for a path, and found it. Slowly, slipping and tugging at his staff, he climbed the bank.

Now for the first time he felt the wind. It went through him with icy fingers, probing at his strength. Clinging to the staff, he plodded on, turning occasionally to be sure the line of trees was at his back.

He thought of what had happened. Who had shot him? An Indian? French Williams? One of the Talrims? Or perhaps some stranger who needed a horse? No matter. There would be time to think about that when he was warm again, and when he had eaten.

Warm? Would he ever be warm again?

He hobbled westward, depending on his staff, and pausing every few steps to ease the pain in his feet. The ground was muddy from the rain, and he had to stop often to shake the mud from his foot coverings.

When he had gone scarcely a mile he found another creek bed and descended into it, pushing through the brush. He scooped up water and drank, then crossed on scattered stones and climbed the far bank.

Every step now was agony, but he plodded on simply because he knew he must not stop. He had thought at moments of giving up, he had thought of surrendering to whatever ill fate awaited him, but it had never really been in him to do so. Somewhere beyond the muddy plain across which he was slogging lay Destination, a place where there was food and warmth, a solution to his immediate problem.

When he fell down again it was at the edge of some

trees. He had come to another creek, and the water still ran north, so he was on the right track. He got up and stumbled to the flat ground under the trees, and here he found the remains of an old campfire.

He searched the ground for something useful, perhaps a broken knife blade, something for a weapon. But what he finally found was a shelter, a lean-to, tightly made and with dry leaves and grass on the ground inside. He fell to his knees, rolled over, and slept.

Words awoke him. He did not open his eyes, for he heard the first words spoken.

"Leave him be, Sarah. He's as good as dead, can't you see?"

"And if he doesn't die?"

"But he will!"

"I'm going to make sure that he does, Paul. I did not come this far to have anything else happen. I want him dead. I want French to have those cattle . . . then there'll be just one man."

"Is it worth it? There are only about two thousand head, Sarah."

"And in Dodge they are worth ten thousand dollars with the outfit."

"Ten thousand? You will have to pay the hands."

"You talk like a fool, Paul. Let me have your gun."

"*My* gun? Why?"

"Because I am going to kill him with it. Then I am going to put the gun in his hand and when he is found they will think he shot himself because of the hopeless situation he was in."

The words of this creature called Sarah came to him clearly and plainly. He was to be murdered, for some reason he did not know. He was not sure whether he could move or not, but he was about to try when Paul spoke again.

"Let's make a fire and have some coffee. I'm cold, Sarah. We can take care of him any time. He isn't going anywhere."

They moved off under a tree and the man built a fire. When they had coffee on and both were sitting down, Tom Chantry lifted his head. The sleep and the emergency had brought clearness to his mind. He looked around cautiously.

Their horses were over there, sixty or seventy yards off.

He eased slowly to his elbows and began to crawl. Moving with infinite care, he made no noise on the sodden ground. Out of the lean-to . . . behind a tree . . . then angling off to come at the horses from the other side.

There was talk between the two at the fire, the smell of coffee . . . He reached the horses, pulled himself up. He got to the brush where they were tied, pulled the loose end of the slipknot, and holding the reins, he grabbed for the pommel. The horse side-stepped away from the smell of him and he fell against the saddle.

He heard an exclamation and made a wild grab for the pommel and caught it. The horse jumped and started to run as his foot reached the stirrup. He fell into the saddle, and then the horse was running and somebody was shooting.

Chapter 10

The horse was a good one, a fast starter, probably somebody's cutting horse. Now it was frightened, and it lunged into a dead run at the first jump. It went through the trees like a jack rabbit, hit the slope, and was up it and topped out on the bank beyond before Chantry could get settled in the saddle.

He took one quick look around and headed the horse westward, where it seemed inclined to go anyway. For half a mile he simply let it run, then eased it down to a trot, held for another half-mile, then a walk and a trot again.

There was no trail that he could make out in the darkness, but he was heading for Trinidad and, weak as he was, he knew nothing under heaven was going to get him off that horse until he reached the town.

It was nothing much when he got there. A few cabins, a scattering of houses and corrals, a few haystacks, and then a saloon or two, a two-story building with a sign that said HOTEL, and a restaurant beyond. A few other places of business were all closed and dark. The street itself was empty.

Still short of the lights he pulled up and swung down, hit the borrowed horse a slap across the rump, and went up the steps and into the hotel.

There were three men in the room. A man wearing a green eye-shade and sleeve garters shuffled and dealt cards at a table alone; another man was behind a desk, and a third sat behind a newspaper at one side of the room.

They all looked up and stared at him. He was sodden with rain. His feet squished as he walked across the floor, leaving mud and water behind him. His hair streaked down over his head, and his cheeks were haggard. The wound on his scalp had reopened and bled.

"I want a room," he said hoarsely, "a room and some food."

"Mister," the clerk protested, "you comin' here like this! You got money to pay for it?"

"I am owner of the herd French Williams just drove through. I was dry-gulched and left for dead. I need that room, mister, and I can pay for it. What I don't need is an argument."

"Now, see here——"

Anger gave him strength, anger and a desperate impatience, for he felt that at any moment he might fall on his face. He reached across the desk and took a handful of the clerk's shirt. "Give me that room—and no more argument!"

"Give it to him." The cool voice was familiar. "I'll stand good for it."

Chantry released his hold and turned half around. Sparrow was walking toward him, folding a newspaper.

"All right," the clerk said grudgingly. "If you say so, Mr. Sparrow."

The cattleman held Chantry by the arm, and took the key the clerk held out. "Come on, young man," he said, "we've got some talking to do."

As they entered the hall to the ground-floor rooms he turned and called back to the gambler, "Mobile, do me a favor and get hold of Sam Baker for me."

The man got to his feet and took his coat off the back of the chair.

Sparrow walked Chantry back to the room, went in, and closed the door behind them. "Get out of those wet clothes," he said. "You need a stiff rubdown and a drink. You get undressed . . . I'll get the drink."

He went out and Chantry dropped to the wooden chair and stooped to pull off the rags of buckskin that hung from his feet. He got one off, and then he pitched over on the floor.

But only for a moment. Slowly, he pushed himself up . . . there was so much to do. He needed a horse. He had to catch up with the herd. He pulled off his buckskin coat and his shirt, both heavy with water. He took the rough towel and began to dry his head and his face and chest. He sat down again, unbuckled his belt and got out of the soaked pants, torn and ragged from his struggles against the brush and the rocks.

Sparrow came back bringing a bottle and a glass, "Get a jolt of this into you. I'm not much of a man for whiskey, but in your condition it's what you need."

Chantry took a gulp of the whiskey and felt the heat of it go all through him. He waited a moment, then took another.

"You get some sleep now," Sparrow said. "We can talk in the morning."

"We'll talk now," Chantry said. "Morning may be too late." He took another gulp of the whiskey, a small one this time. "Somebody tried to kill me." Briefly he told of Sarah and Paul, and the horse he had let loose.

"Do you know them?" Sparrow asked. "I don't."

"Strangers . . . but they knew me. They wanted me—I don't know why." He added, "They didn't look or act like western people . . . from the border states, perhaps."

Sparrow reached into his waistband. He took out a short-barreled .44. "Do you still have a prejudice against using one of these? They'll trace that horse, and they'll find you."

"I just lost my prejudice," Chantry replied shortly. "Give me the gun."

"Keep it close by," Sparrow said.

There was a rap on the door. The gambler named Mobile and another man, somewhat older, stood there.

"Come in," Sparrow said. "Baker, this young man is a friend of mine. He's going to need an outfit, from the skin out, and he'll need it tonight. He'll also need a pistol and a Winchester. Can you open up and get them for him?"

"For you? You're damned right." Baker turned away. Then he glanced over his shoulder. "From the look of him, what he needs is some hot soup . . . a lot of it."

"I'll get it," Mobile said. "It'll have some rain water in it by the time I get back, but it'll be soup and it'll be hot."

Chantry pulled a blanket around him. The liquor and the warmth of the room were taking effect, but he was feeling very tired.

"Sparrow, why are you doing this for me?" he asked. "I thought you had no use for me."

Sparrow smiled, and took a cigar from his pocket. "I didn't," he said, "but you've been moving and you've been making friends. I ran into Koch down in Las Vegas. He hates your guts, but he carries the marks to show why. That was part of it, and then everybody is talking about your deal with French."

"You know about that?"

"Everybody does. That's why I knew you'd need an outfit. I'll have a horse for you, too, the best one I can find."

"Do you think French had me shot?"

"No, that doesn't sound like him. He'd have it done right out in the open where anybody could see it. He's got his own sense of honor about things. He'll steal everything you own, and he'll get you killed in a gun fight if he can, or by a bad horse or a steer, but I doubt he'd ever have a man dry-gulched. Of course, that's just one man's opinion."

Mobile came in with the soup, and he stayed behind after Sparrow left. "You get some sleep," he advised. "I'll kind of set around and keep an eye on things."

"You don't even know me."

Mobile shrugged. "I don't have to. I used to punch cows for Sparrow. I came up the trail with him from Texas, decided that was too rugged a life for a man, and settled down here to deal cards. Contrary to what you might figure, I don't make much more than I would punchin' cows, but I sleep in a bed at night and I don't have to ride drag."

Slowly, carefully, Tom Chantry stretched out on the bed and drew the covers over him. His muscles, stiffened by cold and weariness, slowly relaxed.

"Mobile?" His eyes opened. "Do you know a couple of people named Sarah and Paul?" He went on to describe them, and added, "They'll be hunting that horse, but I've got an idea that horse came from town here, sold to them or rented. He sure wanted to come this way. He was a big bay, about sixteen hands, with three white stockings. It looked like a Pitchfork brand . . . I caught a glimpse as he ran off."

"That's Henry Hazelton's. He's got a ranch outside of town—deals in horses and mules. I've used that horse myself." He took a step toward the door. "Now you get some sleep. I'll ask around."

The door closed, and there was silence in the room. For several minutes Chantry lay quiet, then he got out of bed and limped across the room and propped the chair under the knob. It was an inside room with no window. He closed his eyes. Nothing had ever felt so good as this bed, nothing ever would.

He slept . . . and outside, rain fell upon the town—a rain that drowned the sound of a horse's hoofs splashing through the mud. It smothered the sound of footsteps of a man walking along the alley and trying the back door of the hotel, then entering.

It did not wipe out entirely the sight of a young woman walking across the street and mounting the outside steps of the building across the way.

Mobile, shuffling cards at his table, saw the girl dimly through the rain, saw her put a key in the lock and enter the door. Mobile Callahan trusted neither people nor the appearances of things. Of Tom Chantry he knew nothing beyond the fact that he was respected by Sparrow.

Two people had apparently tried to kill Chantry, one of them a girl, one a man. A girl had just mounted the stairs to the rooms and offices across the way, and it was unlikely that there would be two young women out in the rain on such a night. And where was the man?

This was the only hotel in town, and anyone looking for a homeless man would be likely to come to it. Anyone wishing to kill such a man would not be likely to come by the front door, for he would be seen and remembered.

Mobile made a neat stack of his cards and got to his feet. A glance told him the light in the back hallway was out, and he could smell the faint fumes left by a coal-oil lamp that has recently been blown out. Somebody wanted it dark, and Mobile Callahan was not going to walk along a dark hallway looking for a killer. His mother had raised no foolish children.

His own room was the first on the right side of the hall, Chantry's next to the last on the left side. Mobile stretched and yawned noisily. "Looks like a chance to catch up on some sleep," he said to the clerk. "I think I'll turn in."

He walked back to his room, ignoring the bit of dark hall that lay beyond the light from the lobby, and opened his door. He went in, closing the door, then promptly eased it open a fraction of an inch.

Standing in the darkness with a drawn gun, Mobile listened and heard a faint creak from down the hall, then another. Gently, he eased his door open a little more. By standing tight against the wall he could look along the door and down the passage. At first he could see nothing, and then he made out a darker shadow, and from it a hand that took hold of the knob on Chantry's door and tried it, ever so carefully. Turned it, and pushed . . . nothing happened.

Mobile heard a muffled curse, then the man put a shoulder to the door and lunged against it, but it did not give. Chantry had put a chair under the knob and braced the door.

What happened next was completely unexpected, and ready as Mobile was for almost anything, he was not ready for this.

The man stepped back, drew his gun, and suddenly opened fire.

He held his gun low and Mobile saw the stab of flame in the darkness even as he heard the thunder of the gun in the narrow hall.

Caught flat-footed, it was an instant before he could react, an instant in which the unknown gunman got off at least two shots.

Leaping into the hall, Mobile fired. The gunman wheeled, fired one quick shot at him, and fled. Mobile fired again as the man went through the door.

Doors burst open, the clerk came running. Sparrow, gun in hand, appeared in a door in his long-johns. Mobile ran to him. "He tried to kill him," he said to Sparrow. "I'll light up."

He scarcely noticed the warmth of the lamp chimney as he removed it and applied a match to the wick of the hall lamp.

A dozen men were gathered outside Chantry's door, while Sparrow hammered on it. "Chantry? Are you all right?" he called.

The wall near the door was of one-inch pine boards, and it held three bullet holes. A .44 could penetrate several inches of pine, and the bullets had been fired to strike a man lying on the bed.

For a moment there was no sound inside the room; then a chair scraped on the floor and the door opened. Tom Chantry looked out.

"Are you all right?" Sparrow asked again. As Chantry stepped back, Sparrow entered, followed by Mobile.

"I'm all right. I was lying on my back. If I'd been on my side he'd have gotten me."

Mobile glanced at the bullet holes, then at the wall opposite. In the light from the bedroom lamp he pointed out a bullet buried in a washstand, another that had gone through the wall on the opposite side of the room.

When the others had left, Mobile told about the girl he had seen climbing the steps across the street.

"That's Webb Taylor's office," Sparrow said. "He's an attorney, but so far as I know he's out of town."

After the two men had gone Chantry stretched out once more on the bed. They would not try again—not right away. Hands clasped behind his head, he tried to put things together to make sense.

Out there in the woods the girl had said, "I want French to have those cattle. Then there'll be just one man."

One man? For what? And why did she want French to have the cattle?

He thought and thought, but found no answers, and presently he fell asleep.

Across the street, in the upstairs office, Sarah looked at Paul with disgust. "You fool! Now everybody will know somebody is trying to kill him."

"They'll believe it was French, or that other man we heard about . . . Koch."

She was silent for a few minutes, and then she said, "We've got to stay out of sight, Paul. So you leave town. Now."

"In this rain?"

"They've seen you, Paul. They caught a glimpse of you, anyway. Go up the trail of the cattle. You can be sure Chantry will be coming along, and you can kill him then. But this time don't make a mess of it. Take your time and be sure you get him. Ten thousand dollars may not be all the money in the world, but it is all we're likely to have."

Paul went to the door and peered out. The night was veiled with rain.

"All right," he agreed reluctantly, "I know where there's a shack up the line. I'll stop there." He paused for a moment. "What about you?"

"They know nothing about me. I am just here visiting Webb Taylor and getting some legal advice. You go ahead—and be careful that nobody sees you."

Paul opened the door quickly and went down the stairs, turning at the foot of the steps to walk back to the barn where he had left his horse.

At the back of the building next door and some thirty yards away there were several old boxes and barrels. Crouching among them, and sheltered from the rain, Mobile Callahan, gambler, cowhand, and drifter, watched him go, and looking through the open door of the barn, he saw him lead his horse to the door.

Paul was a slender man about five feet ten, weighing perhaps a hundred and fifty pounds, give or take a few. He wore two belt guns and there was a rifle in the scabbard on his saddle. This horse, too, was from Hazelton's place.

Mobile watched him go, and when he heard the hoofbeats die out, he studied the rooms in the building opposite. There was a lamp lighted now, and occasionally somebody moved back and forth between the light and the window.

After a few minutes he got up and walked back to the hotel. Sparrow was waiting in the lobby.

Mobile told him what he had seen, and Sparrow considered it. Taking two cigars from his pocket, he offered Mobile one of them, then bit the end from the other.

"Mobile," he said slowly, "I've heard it said around the cow camps that you're a good man with a gun."

"That's a reputation I never hunted, Mr. Sparrow, and it's one I don't want."

"I understand that. I don't want just a gun. I want a man with judgment, and you always had that. I want you to ride up the trail and see that Chantry stays alive."

"He's already got one man. He's got Bone McCarthy working for him."

"How do you know that?"

"I saw Bone a while back. He was askin' questions around. I just put two and two together."

"Just the same, I want you to help Chantry get through. I'll pay you two hundred and fifty dollars to stay with him to the railhead."

Mobile drew on his cigar, and looked at Sparrow. He had known Sparrow for going on eight years, and had never known the man to make a foolish or an unnecessary move. "What's your stake in this?" he asked. "Two hundred and fifty dollars—that's seven, eight months' wages for a top hand."

"I have my reasons." Sparrow got to his feet. "You do that, Mobile. I don't want you to get yourself killed, just be around a little while. I think Tom Chantry is riding into more trouble than he can handle. He's a good man. Maybe as good a man as his father was. I want to see him have his chance."

After Sparrow had gone to his room Mobile sat alone in the lobby, drawing on his cigar. Presently he crossed to his table, picked up the deck, and began to deal the cards. He always thought better when he was handling cards.

He shuffled the deck and dealt a hand, then turned them over and looked at them.

Aces and eights ... *black* aces and eights. *The dead man's hand.*

Who was to die? Was it him? Was it Chantry?
Who?

Chapter 11

Tom Chantry opened his eyes and lay still. Slowly it came back to him. The shot out of nowhere, the missing horse, knife, and boots, his struggle to make it through the rain, and then the discovery by the two who intended to kill him . . . why, he didn't know.

He turned his head toward the door. The chair was propped under the knob.

Throwing back the covers, he swung his feet to the floor, but when he tried to stand the pain brought cold sweat to his forehead. Dropping to his knees, he crawled to the door and removed the chair.

When he eased the door open he found several packages wrapped in brown paper. He brought them into the room, and opened them on the bed. A dark red wool shirt, a black handkerchief for his neck, a pair of black jeans, and a wide belt. A couple of suits of underwear, another shirt, socks, and boots. There was also a gun belt and a holster containing a .44 Smith & Wesson, as well as several boxes of cartridges. There was a black, flat-brimmed hat and a fringed buckskin jacket, obviously Indian-made.

The man named Mobile had brought him some salve and bandages the night before and Chantry treated his feet now with the salve, bandaged them, and slipped on the socks.

The day clerk came down the hallway and rapped on the door. Chantry opened it, his right hand holding the pistol.

"No need for that," the clerk said. "I brought you this Winchester. Mr. Sparrow's up and havin' breakfast if you'd care to join him."

"Is Mobile around?"

"Him? He's around somewheres. He's the kind you only see if he's a good mind to have you see him."

Taking the rifle in his hand, Chantry went along the hall to the lobby, and across to the dining room. It was small, with just six oilcloth-covered tables, one of them long enough to seat a dozen, family style.

Hobbling, Chantry crossed the room and sat down opposite Sparrow. "Thanks," he said to the cattleman, "thanks for everything. I don't know why you've done all this, but I appreciate it."

"Better eat while you've got the chance. You're two, maybe three days behind your herd."

"One good day's ride if I have a good horse."

"You'll have one. But don't forget you have enemies." He glanced at the gun on Chantry's hip. "You're wearing a pistol?"

Tom Chantry shrugged. "My sense of what's right and just tells me I shouldn't, but my sense of survival warns me I'd better."

He studied the cattleman. "Aren't you off your beat? I mean, I didn't think you operated this far north."

"Let's just say I was curious. Stories get around, you know, and I heard about your run-in with the Talrims. After our conversation I was wondering how your convictions were matching up with the situation."

"And now you've seen. They've failed."

"Nothing of the kind. You have merely learned that a situation observed from a distance—a safe distance, I might add—is never the same as when met face to face. It is easy to say you do not believe in using guns when you have never faced a gun in the hands of another man, and you unarmed.

"Understand one thing, Mr. Chantry. You can make laws against weapons but they will be observed only by those who don't intend to use them anyway. The lawless can always smuggle or steal, or even make a gun. By refusing to wear a gun you allow the criminal to operate with impunity."

"We have the law."

"But even the law cannot be in your bedroom at night. But there are other things to consider. If you are not to lose your herd you must overtake it, and quickly. Believe me, French Williams will lose no time. He'll drive that herd as he never has before."

"The worst of it is, he may not have far to go."

Sparrow looked at him sharply. "What's that mean?"

"The railroad is building west, and they'll be moving fast."

"You're sure of that?"

"Yes. The only thing I am not sure of is where they are now." He glanced up from his pancakes. "That was my ace in the hole."

After that they ate in silence, but when Chantry finished his coffee and pushed back from the table, Sparrow said, "Understand me, Mr. Chantry. I approve of your stand on guns. Many a man has shot too hastily or been roped into a killing he wishes had never happened. You are wise to restrain your hand, so continue to be wise . . . but not foolish."

"What do I owe you? I mean for the clothes, the outfit?"

"Nothing, if you lose your race. Put it down to the fact that I like a good contest. If you win, I'll give you the bill. Now you'd better be riding."

The horse was a line-back dun, and a good one by the look of it. Mobile Callahan was idling nearby when Chantry came to pick up the horse. A slim, attractive-looking man with cool gray eyes and black hair, he wore a black suit, a fresh white shirt with a black tie, and a black hat. He was wearing a pistol, Chantry noted.

"I've been through the town, Chantry," he said, "and that Paul, whatever-his-name-is, has flown the coop. The girl's still here, but I've a hunch if they tried twice they will try again, so watch your step."

Tom Chantry mounted and turned his horse toward the old Santa Fe Trail. The trail went north by east, but French Williams knew this country well and he might drive further to shorten the trail to Dodge.

When he had gone scarcely more than a mile from town he swung from the trail, but when he had again gone no more than a mile he swung back toward it, scouting for sign as he rode. But he saw no tracks made since the rain.

He was remembering things his father had taught him. At the time he had not thought of it as being taught. But on many occasions his father had often pointed out things along the trail, or told him stories of Indians and Indian fighting and trailing.

"If you're in risky country," he used to say, "don't let 'em set you up. Swing off your trail, change directions, keep 'em worried so they can't lay for you. And study the sign. Watch wild animals and birds, they'll tell you plenty. Most of all, trust to your horse, particularly if he's from wild stock. If there's anybody around, a horse will know it."

His father had never seemed to be teaching, and yet when he thought of it now he realized that Borden Chantry had said things that counted. "If you want to live easy in your mind, son," he used to say, "be sure folks respect you. Saves a lot of trouble."

He was riding warily, alive to every shadow, every suspicion of movement. He avoided places where a man might easily lie in wait, and several times he changed direction.

So it was that he glimpsed the pony tracks. They were off his line of travel, but his eyes caught a certain roughness in the grass and he swung his horse over to have a better look.

Unshod ponies . . . at least six, perhaps more. He knew he was no match for six warriors of the Kiowa or Comanche tribes. Deliberately he turned his mount away, back-tracking them.

He had gone no more than a quarter of a mile when he saw where the riders had drawn up their horses and stayed for several minutes, partly screened by a thick patch of willows and young cottonwoods. They had all been facing toward the wall of brush, obviously looking over it. At what? Not at him, for he had not come that way.

Sitting his horse where they had sat theirs, he looked over the brush and could see nothing but a barren slope, empty of life.

He found an opening in the wall of brush, worked his way through, and scouted the slope. Sure enough, he came upon the tracks of a lone horseman who had ambled along the slope unaware of the Indians watching him from cover.

Tom Chantry back-tracked the rider, and saw that the tracks showed frequent hesitations, as though the rider had somebody under observation or was scouting a trail. Suddenly Tom realized the rider had been watching *him!* And now that rider was being stalked by Indians.

Who could it be? Was this the man called Paul? Whoever it was, he now had problems of his own and Tom Chantry decided to let him deal with them as best he could.

Keeping to open country, avoiding possible ambush spots, he rode hard, occasionally veering to confuse any watcher, his one idea being to catch up with the drive.

The herd's tracks were there, but they were a day or two old . . . it was difficult to tell for sure. Obviously, French was taking advantage of Chantry's disappearance and was making time.

Tom Chantry was becoming aware of something else. There was movement among the Indians. He came upon their sign several times, parties riding unshod ponies crossed the cattle trail, riding east, small parties riding to become one big party, gathering in the direction to which the cattle must be driven.

Was it the cattle they were after? Or a drive upon the buffalo hunters in the Panhandle area? Or an effort, a last effort perhaps, to stop the rails?

He slowed his pace. He must not encounter such a party, for if they were bound for an attack for any of those reasons they would not hesitate to kill him en route.

By sundown the tracks of the cattle were fresher, and the cattle drive had veered toward the east, perhaps only to reach a water hole.

Chantry circled a low hill, studying carefully for tracks, and when he saw none that went up the hill he made his way to the crest. There were boulders and low brush as well as half a dozen trees there, the only cover he had found in some distance. From the summit he could study the country all about in the last light.

To the west there was nothing; it was broken, empty country with mountains rimming the skyline. All around him the horizon was empty, except that off to

the northeast there was the faint glow of what must be
a fire . . . the cattle herd?

He was about to leave the hill when he heard, off in
the distance, a burst of firing. Stare as he might, he
could make out nothing, and he had swung into the
saddle preparatory to riding off the hill when he
heard a pound of hoofs.

For several minutes he saw nothing, and then it
was a lone rider, coming fast, low over his saddle. He
swept by, turning toward the direction of the herd, and
was scarcely past when a band of Indians, riding hard,
followed.

There were at least six in the bunch—in the now
vague light he could not be sure of their number. He
waited a moment longer, listening, and then rode down
the hill and headed north.

As he rode he made his decision. The thing to do
was not to join the herd but to let the herd join him. He
would ride ahead, make a dark camp somewhere along
the line of travel the drive must follow, and when they
came up to him, he would join them . . . in daylight,
when there would be no mistakes.

To the north there had seemed to be a low rim of
darkness . . . a line of trees? The river? He knew the
Purgatoire took a bend somewhere ahead of him, and
it was probably the trees along that stream, partly hidden by the depth of the river bed.

How far had he come? His route had see-sawed
back and forth so often that he had lost track of distance in his effort to avoid an ambush. Probably he
was no more than sixteen or seventeen miles from Trinidad.

In the gathering dark he continued his way north,
growing more and more wary as he neared the river.
Several times he drew up to listen into the night, but
he heard no sound except the faint rustle of wind.

The first stars appeared. The ground fell away slightly and he saw the dark wall of the trees. Descending into the river bottom, he could feel the coolness rising
from the water. He walked his horse along in the darkness, every sense keyed for trouble.

He had drawn his pistol as he went under the trees,

and he allowed the horse to go forward to find his own way, which it seemed to be doing without hesitation, ears pricked and alert.

He was apparently on some sort of trail, for the horse's hoofs fell evenly, and the dun held to a good, fast walk. Suddenly water gleamed gray before him.

The dun stopped and its head came up. It seemed about to whinny when Chantry spoke sharply but softly. *"No!* Steady, boy! Steady!"

Although the dun jerked its head impatiently, it made no sound.

Then he caught the smell . . . *woodsmoke.* Somebody, somewhere quite near, had a fire going.

The smell was faint, but with it there was something more. Coffee . . . !

Chantry, gun in hand, walked the dun forward toward the gray water, toward the fire he could not see.

Chapter 12

There is a subtle awareness in the night. The darkness around you does not sleep; it is awake, alert, sensing. It is alive to movement, and feels the changes in the air, the smell, the temperature.

The trees are aware, and the bushes. The birds and small animals are aware, and they listen, hesitant, suspecting. Awareness of danger is an element of their being. It is like their breathing, like the blood in their veins, and one who lives much with the wilderness becomes so aware, too. Living with stillness, he detects sounds unheard by the casual passers-by, sees things they do not see, catches odors too faint for their nostrils. Half of woodcraft is attention, and all of survival.

Tom Chantry had been bred in the West, and in the East he had spent much time in the woods, but what was happening to him now was different, strange and exciting. For the first time he was not *in* the night, but was a *part* of the night. He had come in recent days of scouting, riding, suffering, and struggle to a point where he belonged to all this.

Only a short time ago he had ridden, unseeing, past things that seemed of no importance to him, but now he sensed them. His ear was learning the difference between a movement of the wind and that of a small animal or bird. His eye was quick to catch the difference between a bird that flew up from fear and one going about its usual business. He could detect, by the changes in temperature, hollows or creek beds before he came up to them, for they were cooler in this weather, more humid.

Chantry walked his horse a few steps, then drew up, waiting.

He felt a faint stir from the wind, lost the scent of coffee for a moment, found it again. He heard no sound,

and he felt that the man who had the fire was moving
silently or was listening. The scent of the coffee was
enough to tell him the man was awake.

A slight dampness, a coolness, coming to his right
cheek indicated a hollow or a spring close by. He turned
his mount ever so slightly and edged it through the
trees. His gun was still in his hand, and he was ready.

It might, of course, be the Talrims, but he did not
think so. They would be closer to the herd, watching
for him, or carrying out whatever they meant to do.
Whoever it was, he was prepared.

The gleam of the fire caught his eye, and there it
was, not twenty feet off, in a hollow below some brush.
He drew up again and waited. When he at last heard a
sound, it was a voice.

"Welcome to my fire. I am Sun Chief."

The Indian materialized from the shadows and Tom
Chantry dismounted, holding out his hand, and the
Pawnee took it.

"There is coffee. In the light I would look for you,
but you find me first."

He took Chantry's dun and stripped the saddle from
it, picketing the horse in a small glade close by. Then
he came back to the fire, where Chantry had already
filled his cup.

"How did you know I was around?" Tom asked.

The Pawnee shrugged. "I know you come. And on
the road I met the man from Trinidad—the one called
Moby."

Moby? Mobile? But what would the gambler be doing out here?

"He told me you were coming."

There were other things to consider, and Chantry put
aside the question of Mobile Callahan's movements.
"What about the railroad?" he asked.

"Three days maybe, for the cows. The Pawnee
filled his cup and Chantry shared the food from his
saddlebags. "If there is no trouble."

"Where is the herd?"

Sun Chief pointed. "Where the creek begins. The
creek called Caddoa."

Knowing nothing of that creek, Chantry inquired, "How far from here?"

The Pawnee gestured toward the north. "Not far. I show you."

The campsite the Indian had chosen was a good one. It was under the edge of a cut that dropped off to a creek bed, but was some twenty feet back from the river and at least ten feet above it. There would have been room for one more man and his horse.

When the Indian had smoked he crawled into his blankets, and only then did he tell Chantry one last thing. "There are Kiowas at Big Timbers. The Cheyennes and Arapahoes have gone."

Kiowas at Big Timbers? And Big Timbers lay between his herd and the railroad. If the Cheyennes and Arapahoes had left such a favorable camping ground there must be a reason. Were the Kiowas planning an attack in which the others did not want to be involved?

Big Timbers . . . why did the name sound a bell? Perhaps because of a story his father had told him long ago, or some chance phrase remembered from a conversation in his home when men had talked of the far plains and the shining mountains, the forests where no man had walked. The name had a special sound to it. *Big Timbers . . . ?*

At breakfast they ate jerky and drank coffee, Chantry inquired about Big Timbers, and listened to Sun Chief tell in a few phrases what he knew.

"Big trees . . . what you call *alamo* . . . cottonwood. Fourteen miles long it was, but many cut for logs or fires . . . no brush around . . . only grass. Springs and streams . . . a place the Indian likes. Big powwows held there . . . fights, too. It is a good place."

So it undoubtedly was, but the trouble-hunting Kiowas had taken away its charm for Tom Chantry.

They had ridden no more than a mile in the morning sunlight when Sun Chief pointed across the tawny slopes at black dots circling against the pale sky. "Buzzards. Something dead."

"Or dying," Chantry said. "We will see."

They rode on, their horses' hoofs beating on the drying turf. When they topped out on the rise below the buzzards they saw a man's body, stripped and bloody lying in the hollow beyond.

Riding down swiftly, they drew up close to it. Streaked with bloody gashes, it lay there, an ugly thing under the flat sky.

Tom Chantry passed the reins to Sun Chief and stepped down, fighting his repugnance. He turned the body over. It was Paul, and he was not dead. His body twitched and his fluttering eyes opened wide.

"I did not even see them," he said distinctly. "It was sundown, and I was looking for you."

"We'll take you to the herd," Chantry said. "They're pretty handy with wounds."

Paul's eyes stared blankly. "I shouldn't have listened to her. I should never have come. I never wanted money that much, but she did. She wanted money, or she wanted blood . . . I was never sure."

Chantry knelt and started to slip an arm under him. *"No!"*

He stopped, waiting, but whatever Paul had been about to say was smothered in the blood that came from his mouth. He rolled over on his side, choking and gasping. "No," he managed again . . . and died.

Chantry pulled a handful of dry grass and wiped the blood from his fingers. He looked at the body, and then walked to his horse.

He started to speak. "If we had a shovel . . ."

"No time," Sun Chief said. "We ride."

He pointed. Two hills away were Indians, a dozen of them, coming toward them.

Chantry turned his mount, and riding beside each other, they moved away, trotting their horses, not running them.

The Indians came on riding faster now. Chantry drew his rifle from the scabbard, letting them see the shine of it.

"No shoot," Sun Chief said, but he was showing his own rifle.

The Indians came up to the body and drew up, looking after them.

They saw the fire before they reached the cattle. The herd was bunched for the night, and the men were around the chuck wagon, except for those on night herd and one man on a high knoll as lookout.

The herd was bunched in the open, the remuda held near a small patch of trees and brush.

Helvie was first to see Chantry. He looked from Chantry to Sun Chief, and back again. "Figured we'd seen the last of you," he said dryly. "What happened?"

"I got dry-gulched," Chantry answered.

"It wasn't him," Helvie said quickly. "He ain't left the herd."

"Didn't think it was. That doesn't seem to be his style."

"You're smarter'n I thought."

French Williams was standing near the fire, watching as they rode in. "Howdy!" he said. "Better eat up. We're making a night drive."

"Where to?"

"South and west. There's a bunch of Kiowas north of here."

"Heard of them." Chantry poured coffee. "They got you buffaloed?"

Williams turned his head quickly. "No. It's the wisest thing to do, that's all."

Chantry sipped his coffee. "They know you're here," he said, "so you aren't fooling anybody. They can catch up any time they've a mind to. And," he added, "there's bunches of Indians south of here, too."

"What's on your mind?"

"Go north," Chantry said, "right past Big Timbers. No sense in letting them think we're afraid of them."

"All right," Williams replied carelessly. "It might just work. If they ride out to talk, you going to make palaver with them?"

"I might," Chantry replied.

"You do it," Williams said. "I'd like to see how an eastern gent gets along with Indians." He glanced at Sun Chief. "Where'd you find him?"

"He's been working for me right along," Chantry answered calmly. "He was one of Frank North's Pawnee scouts."

"I know him," French Williams said. "He's a damn good man."

Suddenly a thought came to Chantry. "French," he asked, "does anybody want you dead?"

"Me? Maybe fifty people. Why?"

"Somebody tried to kill me, somebody I don't know. I don't have any enemies that I can think of and nobody stands to gain if I die."

"Why tie it to me?"

"There was a mention that if I was dead there'd only be one more. Now, I don't share anything with anybody but you."

"The herd?"

Chantry shrugged. "I can't think of anything else."

"What about your pa? Somebody killed him. With you back west again they might think you've come out here to wind that up."

"It isn't likely. That was a long time ago."

Both of them were silent for a minute, and Tom listened abstractedly to the mutter of conversation around the fire.

"Anyway," he added, "the girl wanted money. That's what Paul said."

"Paul?"

"The girl called him that." Then, concisely, Chantry told his experiences of the past few days: the dry gulching, his escape, the attempted killing in Trinidad . . . and Sparrow.

"What's he doing in this?" French Williams asked. "I don't figure Sparrow."

"He said he wanted to see how I'd manage without using a gun."

"That don't make sense. I know Sparrow. He's a no-time-for-fooling-around man. I never knew him to do anything like this before." French looked at him quickly. "Is he any relation of yours?"

"No."

"Then it certainly don't make sense. Unless," he added, "he figures to pick up the herd himself."

Chantry got up and threw the dregs of his coffee into the buffalo-chip fire. "I think it concerns you and me," he said, "and nobody else."

As he walked to the wagon for his bedroll, he glanced at the men, somber over their coffee, speaking little, their rough-hewn, unshaven faces thrown into relief by the firelight. They were a solid, capable lot. Even the bad ones were good men with the cattle, hard workers to a man . . . Suddenly, for the first time he felt a kinship with these men who shared with him what would in the East be considered as nothing less than an adventure. Here it was the day's work, and little different from any other day's.

All of them knew the Kiowas were out there, and every man among them knew the Kiowas for fearless, dreaded fighters, yet they were prepared to ride on, right past their encampment—or through it if necessary.

Some of these men were of a sort he might never have encountered had he not come west, and they were, in some cases, men whom he would not have chosen for friends, but when trouble showed they would be men who would stand by until death, if need be. For the first time he clearly understood what Sparrow had told him, what Lambert meant, and the others who had tried to tell him what the West was like.

These were hard, lonely men, driven by no man knew what impulses, what secret dreams or thoughts, and they came from all walks of life, all kinds of backgrounds. There was no pattern beyond the one of hardihood and courage.

"You know, French," he said, when he went back to the fire, "no matter how it turns out, I'll have learned a lot on this trip. I wouldn't have missed it for anything."

French looked up, a sudden smile on his face. "Maybe we'll ride another trail, my friend, another trail besides this. You've come a long way since that night in Cimarron."

Yes . . . yes, he had. But how much further was he to go? It might be no further than the camp of the Kiowas, nor as far as the railhead.

There was not much time left, not many days, not many miles, and then he would know.

Chapter 13

Dawn broke cold and gray. Tom Chantry rolled out of his blankets, scrambled into his clothes, and tugged on his boots.

Helvie and McKay were at the wagon, plates held out for the cook. Chantry stood up, stamped his feet into his boots, and slung his gun belt around his waist. Helvie looked at it, but made no comment.

Rugger strolled up to the wagon, throwing a sour glance at the gun. "You strap that on an' you may have to use it."

"If I have to, I will," Chantry said, and he added, "When this drive's over, Rugger, if you have any money to bet, I'll outshoot you for whatever you've got."

Rugger stared at him. "Huh! You must think you're good. I'll take that bet."

French Williams rolled out and sat up. "You'd better not, Rugger. I think Chantry can shoot. I think he'll surprise the hell out of you."

Rugger snorted, but he was less confident. If French thought Chantry could shoot, it was a good bet that he could. For French Williams made few mistakes in such matters.

"French, do you know Clay Spring?" Chantry asked.

"I been there a time or two. I guess everybody in this country knows it."

"How about stopping there tonight?"

"I'd sort of figured on it."

Williams was a neat, natty man who looked well in whatever he wore. This morning he wore a blue army shirt, black jeans, and a flat-brimmed hat. His boots were almost new, and were decorated with large-roweled Mexican spurs. He wore his gun tied down. Chantry suspected that Williams had a better background than was implied by his conversation or by his way of life.

"That man the Indians killed?" Williams asked now. "You say his name was Paul?"

"Yes."

Williams walked away without comment.

Within minutes the herd was on the move, pointed east now. The dust beneath the hoofs of the cattle rose in clouds. The sky remained dull, leaden.

Clay Spring, if Chantry remembered rightly what he had been told, lay at the foot of a mesa where several runoff springs combined to form Clay Creek. He had never been there, but Bone McCarthy had mentioned it.

From there they would drive to the vicinity of Two Buttes, and this would be what the Kiowas would expect. But their next move would, he believed, surprise the Indians. It might also confuse them. For instead of driving away to avoid the Indians, they would drive right toward them. And he had his own ideas about what to do next.

Oddly enough, he had come to like French. The arrogant gunman, with his amused, taunting eyes, puzzled him, but Chantry wasted no time in trying to figure out his personality. His liking stemmed from the fact that Williams was good at his job, and Tom Chantry always admired a man who knew what he was doing and did it well.

The thought came to him that he might have to kill Williams, but if so he would do it with regret. That thought gave him pause. He . . . kill? Such an idea had been foreign to him, but now he was considering the possibility, if there was no other way out.

His readiness to accept the possible necessity of it worried him. He must guard his emotions and his actions all the more now. He must not only be wary of others, but of himself.

In spite of the dust, there was a feeling in the air that he liked, a smell from the land. Eastward the rising sun shone in the faces of the cattle. They walked stolidly on, sometimes trotted a little, then walked again.

Today he stayed with the herd, interested to see how

easily his horse responded to the work, and how accustomed to it he himself had become. His hand was sure, his movements easy . . . he had changed.

But he must not permit the ready smile of French Williams to put him off. Why had Williams so easily accepted the idea of going north into the face of the Kiowas? Did he think Chantry would fail when he faced them and lose the herd there? Or had Williams already approached the Kiowas, perhaps on a share-and-share-alike basis? It would not be the first time Indians had raided a herd or a wagon train at the instigation of a white man.

As he rode, his thoughts returned to the girl called Sarah. Of the two, the girl had been the stronger, the most dangerous. And she was an attractive woman with a good figure, enough to take the eye of any man, east or west, but this was the West, where women were scarce.

He had been thinking there must be some connection between them and Williams, but Williams had seemed to know nothing about them.

The cattle went ahead steadily, heads swinging to the rhythm of their walk. The cowhands lounged in their saddles, thinking of the campfire ahead, the strong black coffee, and the warm food.

Tom Chantry swung out from the flank where he had been riding, and loped his horse along the slope of the low hill. Clay Creek Spring was not far ahead, hidden in a notch of hills. Below it was a holding ground, somewhat higher than the ground around it, a pleasant place for the cattle.

A bird flew up, from almost under his horse's hoofs. The saddle creaked, his spurs jingled, and he topped out on the rise.

The three Indians came out on the ground around him without warning. They had been lying down, horses concealed beyond the rise, and their dusky bodies blended with the brown earth and the growing shadows. He heard the explosion of a gun, felt the jolt of it in his fist, then the hammer fell again and he saw an Indian spin and fall, the knife dropping from his hand.

An arm came around Chantry's throat from behind,

and he knew, instinctively, a knife would be in the other hand. He kicked his boots free of the stirrups and threw himself from his horse.

Hitting the ground with a thump, he rolled over, and jolted free of the Indian. He came to his feet quickly, just as the warrior, knife held low, sprang at him. He was a big man, tall as Chantry, and equally broad in the shoulders.

The Indian crouched, then came in. Chantry moved swiftly, and with the ease of long practice, a practice he had never used until now except in friendly wrestling matches. His left palm slapped the Indian's knife-wrist to his right and out of line with his body, his right hand grabbed the wrist, and he stepped across in front of the Kiowa and threw him over, hard.

The Indian hit the ground, but he retained his grip on his knife, and came up fast. The man was like a big cat; his black eyes gleamed as he circled to come in again.

Chantry's gun lay where it had fallen, several feet away. His horse, the blue roan, had trotted off to one side and stopped, the red sunset on his saddle.

The Indian's hand was lower now . . . he was a wily fighter, not to be taken by the trick again.

"You are a brave man," Tom Chantry heard himself say. "I shall hate to kill you."

Did the man understand? Chantry heard him suck breath and then he came in swiftly, slashing right and left with the knife. Chantry side-stepped to his left to put the Indian out of position, but the warrior turned abruptly and lunged again.

Chantry sprang back, but in his boots he was not agile enough, and as he went back he tripped over the body of one of the other Indians. His opponent lunged forward, but off balance, and tripped over Chantry.

Tom sprang to his feet, more quickly this time, and kicked savagely at the Indian's head. The boot heel glanced off the Indian's temple and sent him rolling.

Leaping on him, Chantry slipped an arm under him and across the warrior's throat, clapping the palm of his right hand against the Indian's skull, his left hand grasping his own right arm in a strangle hold. He knew he could kill the Indian now, and he put on pressure, fighting for his life.

Suddenly horses were all around them, and Williams was saying, "Step back, Chantry. I've got a gun on him."

Slowly Tom Chantry released his hold and stepped away from the Indian, who lay gagging and choking, and then slowly the brave got to his feet.

Rugger was there, and Helvie and McKay; there were four guns on the Indian, and Rugger eared back his hammer. "I'll kill him!" he yelled. "I'll—"

"No!" Chantry snapped the word. "You kill him, and you'll have to kill me."

He turned to face the Indian. "I am Tom Chantry," he said. "You fought well. Go in peace."

The Indian looked at him, then at the others.

"You going to let him go?" Helvie asked in astonishment.

Suddenly Sun Chief was there beside them. He held out Chantry's pistol and Tom took it, dropping it into his holster.

"He goes free," he said. "He's too good a man to shoot down."

Rugger swore. "He's nothin' but a damn redskin. He'll kill you the first chance he gets."

"Maybe. But in the meantime he goes free." He spoke to Sun Chief. "Tell him he can go. Tell him I shall come to the village under the Big Timbers to see him . . . soon."

"No need to tell. He knows what you say." The Pawnee's rifle was in his hands. "That's He-Who-Walks-With-Wolves, but often he is called Wolf Walker. He is a big warrior."

"Let him go."

Wolf Walker looked at him a moment, then deliberately he turned on his heel and walked away.

French Williams looked at the two dead Indians and commented dryly to Rugger: "You'd better copper your bets, Rug. That's as good shooting as I've ever seen, left and right, both dead center."

"It was luck," Chantry said. "They surprised me. Came right up off the ground."

"So you just killed two of them with two shots, and then whipped Wolf Walker bare-handed—and him with a knife. Mister, you call it what you want to, only don't call it luck."

Sun Chief caught up the blue roan and Chantry swung into the saddle. As they started back toward the herd, Helvie rode alongside Chantry and held out his hand. "Whatever I may have thought about you back at the start, I take it back. Next time you need a hand, you just call my name and I'll come a-runnin' . . . no matter where you want to go."

"Because I was able to handle those Indians?"

"No, sir. I don't regard that. It was the way you let Wolf Walker go. That shines, mister!"

The cattle passed over the end of the mesa in the last moments of light, all shades of hide lost in a uniform darkness. The hands circled them to a stop on the flat below Clay Creek Spring, and the chuck wagon lumbered over the rocks and swung into place. While Dutch unhitched for him, the cook lowered the back of the wagon to make his table, and began setting out the grub.

Tom Chantry gathered sticks from the remains of old campfires and, using dry grass and leaves for tinder, got a small fire started. He added buffalo chips and hunted out some dried brush.

It was a good camp—the best camp so far, Tom thought. Rugger was surly, and Kincaid still avoided him, but Dutch, Helvie, and McKay were friendly and easy. The fire burned brightly, and the food tasted good. For the first time in days, Tom was not hurting anywhere, and now he had a good feeling about the fight with Wolf Walker. He did not think about the two Indians he had killed. They had attacked him without warning, and his reaction had been immediate and instinctive.

French Williams was curious. "Now, that shootin'," he commented, "surely didn't look like the work of a man who never used a gun."

"I never said I had never used a gun," Chantry replied simply. "Pa was a good hand, as you know, and he started teaching me early. I've always had a knack

. . . good coordination, I guess. I've hunted a good bit, and shot up a lot of ammunition at targets. Up there" —he jerked his head back toward the scene of the fight—"was the first time I'd tried to get a gun out fast in a long time."

"We heard the shots," McKay commented, "just *boom-boom,* almost like one sound."

Chantry glanced over at Williams. "How far is it to Two Buttes?"

"Fourteen, fifteen miles, I'd guess. I never did ride directly from here to there. We'll make a proper day of it."

All the men were tired, but the last events of the day had excited them and stirred them to conversation. Chantry leaned back against his bedroll and listened to Helvie, who was telling of a famous fight back in 1867, a running battle between Indians and the riders of a stage headed for the Big Timbers station.

From that the talk continued—talk of cattle and buffalo, of the stage lines and the Santa Fe Trail. Finally Tom carried his bedroll into the shadows near the wagon, and pulling off his boots and his gun belt, he rolled in and slept.

His last memories were of the occasional crackle of the fire and the low murmur of conversation.

When he opened his eyes the fire was down to the last red coals. All the men were asleep except those with the cattle. He was about to turn over and go back to sleep when he saw Rugger slip from his bed and move off into the darkness. Something about his manner moved Chantry to watch him go—not toward the horses, but off into the darkness, obviously anxious not to be seen.

Where was he going? And for what reason?

Chapter 14

For a moment Chantry thought of following him,
then decided the man was probably just going into the
woods on some business of his own, and Chantry turned
over and went to sleep again.

But in the morning he remembered this small inci-
dent, and when he had belted on his gun and stepped
into his boots he glanced around.

Rugger was saddling a horse, as were Helvie, Mc-
Kay, and Kincaid, getting ready to ride out and relieve
the night guards. He saddled his own horse, and waited
until they had gone. Then, leaving the dun at camp, he
went into the woods where he had seen Rugger go.

He had no trouble in picking up a track. A heel
print here, a kicked stone there . . . for a hundred yards
he trailed him back into the brush and scattered juniper, and then across the slope of a hill. There the faint
trail went down into the hollow beyond.

Here the trail ended. Near a flat rock there were two
cigarette butts.

For several minutes Tom Chantry stood there, trying
to puzzle it out. Rugger was not exactly a contempla-
tive man, not the sort who would walk all this way to be
alone with his thoughts. He had come for a reason.

Chantry looked around. Due east lay the trail to Two
Buttes, an open stretch of valley two or three miles
wide, and easy going, bordered on the south by Two
Buttes Creek. About five or six miles away lay the
Santa Fe Trail, or one branch of it. Two Buttes, the
highest of which lifted about three hundred feet above
the surrounding country, were dimly visible on the
horizon.

Nothing else. . . .

He had turned away when he saw, in the shelter of
another rock, a place where a small fire had been built.

Not for warmth, for the man had not sat near it, and it was built so that it would be visible only from the valley below.

A signal then. But to whom?

There were no other tracks, so if he had expected anyone to meet him, that person had not arrived.

Had he left any word there?

Carefully, searching with this fresh idea in mind, Chantry looked around, and suddenly he saw it, near where the fire had been . . . a tobacco sack. Picking it up, he felt something inside and opened it . . . there was a page torn from a tally book, and on it, written in a clumsy hand, these words

2 Butes

Big Timbers

Kiwas at Big Timbers

He returned the note to the sack and replaced it. Then he walked back to get his horse.

The others had eaten, and the chuck wagon was packed and ready. The cook turned to glance at him, then gestured toward the seat. "I put some grub an' coffee out for you. Figured you'd be hungry."

"Thanks."

The cook waited while he ate, and presently he said, "I like your style, Chantry. Can't say I cottoned to you right off, but you've shaped up."

"Thanks," Tom said again.

"What's goin' on? I don't like it a-tall, the way things are. French ain't like himself, an' there's hard feelin' among the boys . . . like they were up to something they didn't care for."

Chantry finished eating, cleaned the plate with sand, and passed it to the cook. "You can't lose, Cookie," he said. "Either French or I will pay you boys off if we get through with the herd."

"They tell me you're figurin' to drive right through Big Timbers."

"Why not? Look, if the Kiowas want us they can ride up on us any time. By driving in any other direction we still couldn't get away—cattle move too slow. If they mean to attack, we can't avoid it. So why not take the quickest way, where there's the best water and grass? Why not drive right at them so they know we're not afraid? We know where they are, and they know we know, so they'll be wary of a trap. They'll be sure we've got reason for being confident. Anyway, I never found that a man could avoid trouble by running away from it."

He waited while the wagon pulled out and started over the ridge. When it was lined out on the trail, he rode south to the banks of a creek that flowed into the Two Buttes almost due south of Clay Spring.

The banks were cloaked with shrub willows, many of them growing ten to fifteen feet high. He went in among them, drew up there, and stepped down from the saddle searching for a vantage point from which he could watch the rock on the hillside where the message had been left.

From time to time he looked toward the herd, now only a dust cloud down the long valley. He drank at the stream, and let his horse browse on the rich green grass along the bank.

An hour passed. Just as he was about to step into the saddle again, he heard the beat of hoofs. From over the ridge behind him came two riders, who cantered down the slope, splashed through the shallow stream, and went up the opposite slope to where the message had been left.

They were some distance off, but he needed no closer view to know who they were. The Talrims!

The Talrims and Rugger in this . . . and who else?

But the message? What did it mean? 2 Butes was obvious enough, and it was their next stop. After that they were going to Big Timbers, though not in one long drive. And at Big Timbers there were Kiowas.

Rugger was apparently telling the Talrims their direction of travel, and warning them about the Kiowas at Big Timbers. But what else? Despite himself, Chantry was worried. There might be some other meaning which he did not grasp, some other reason for the message.

When the two riders had disappeared over the ridge in the direction of Clay Spring, he rode out of the willows and followed the herd.

The drive to Two Buttes was an easy one, and Chantry rode the drag all the last half. They bunched the cattle on the plain north of the Buttes, avoiding the breaks along the canyon that lay just to the south.

Twice during the last part of the drive they saw Indians. Two of them sat on a ridge watching, apparently unworried about being seen. That night the camp was quiet.

"What do you think, French?" Akin said at last. "Will they tackle us?"

Williams shrugged. "Maybe yes, maybe no. From what I hear, that passel of Kiowas shapes up like a war party, and if they want beef there isn't any closer than we are. The same goes for scalps. They know they've tackled my drives a couple of times with no luck, so that may steer 'em off, but I doubt it."

"I think we're in for a fight," McKay agreed.

Chantry sipped his coffee, listened to the talk, and watched Rugger. When he had finished eating, Rugger strolled over to where Kincaid was repairing a broken bridle. For several minutes they talked in low tones, and nobody seemed to be paying any attention. Williams was lying on his back, his hat over his eyes.

Rugger and Kincaid were two of Williams' boys . . . did Williams know what was going on? Was this a part of a plan? The Talrims had kept pace with them for days, and Chantry was sure they were Williams' ace in the hole. A shoot-out at the last minute; and with Chantry dead the cattle belonged to Williams.

Suddenly he remembered the girl Sarah . . . where did she figure in all of this? Did she know that Paul was dead? Had she given up whatever she was trying to do?

She had wanted Tom Chantry dead because then only one man would stand between her and what she wanted, and that one man had to be French Williams. Yet French professed to know nothing about her . . . or was it Paul? Had he ever mentioned Sarah's name to French?

He suddenly said to French, "We've never talked about your background."

Williams' eyes were level and cold. "And we are not planning to," he said.

"I was thinking about Paul," Chantry went on. "We need not talk about it, but you had better do some thinking about it."

"I do not know anyone named Paul."

"And there was the girl named Sarah," Chantry continued.

Williams stared at him. "Sarah? Sarah and Paul? It can't be."

"Those were the names. They spoke of killing me, and then added that there would be only one man left. Williams, the only thing you and I have in common are those cattle. If both of us die before we get to the railhead, who gets the cattle?"

The cynical amusement was gone from Williams' eyes. His face looked drawn.

"You wouldn't have gotten to Dodge," he said, "so the cattle would belong to me. And if I died . . . no, it is absurd! I can't believe it."

"Sarah would be nineteen or twenty," Chantry said; "Paul a few years older."

"And Paul is dead? The Kiowas killed him?"

"Yes."

"Then it is over," he muttered, half to himself. "That will be an end to it."

"I don't think so," Chantry insisted quietly. "The girl was the stronger one. She was the one who was pushing hardest. Without her I don't believe Paul would have done anything; nor do I believe she will quit."

Williams stared at Tom. "I thought they had forgotten me," he said. "Now they find me again, and it is for this!"

They were alone—the others had gone out on night guard, or were asleep. "I wanted to go back some day," Williams said gloomily. "It is not a place to forget. My boyhood was there, and where a man has lived as a boy . . . he has feelings for it."

"My first home was out here somewhere," Chantry said. "I never knew exactly where . . . I think it was over east of here. You know how it is . . . plains are plains; and afterward my mother never would talk about it. Pa was well-off until that norther wiped him out and we had to move into town."

"I always wanted to go back," Williams said. "I had a good time as a boy."

"You can always go back."

"You have much to learn, my friend. No one ever really goes back, for when you return you are not the same as when you left, and everything is different, and strange. You look about where everything ought to be familiar, but nothing is right. I know, my friend. But still I did want to go back."

"What have Sarah and Paul to do with it?"

Williams shrugged. "Perhaps nothing. But I do not think there is much to go back to if they have come so far to kill me. . . . Yes, I know them. They are the children of my cousin. With me, they are the last of our line. My father always told me I should avoid them. . . . They were no good, he said, and he should know, for he came of the same family."

"What about your mother and father?"

"Dead. My mother died when I was very small— my father only a few years ago. My mother was lovely . . . she came of an old, old line. My father was a common soldier who rose from the ranks to become an officer. That is not an easy thing to do in the French Army. As a boy he dreamed of going off to India, of becoming a general.

"Actually he served in Africa, and lost an arm there. He came home then, married my mother, and bought a farm . . . call it an estate if you will. His own family he did not like, and he avoided my mother's family as well.

"They had refused to sanction the marriage until it became obvious that my mother would refuse to obey, and then they sanctioned it, but unwillingly. Later, after my father was visited by some of France's foremost military men, their attitude changed, but he was a proud man and would have none of it.

"He had the devil's own temper, and my own was like it. When I was not yet sixteen the arrogant nephew of an important man demanded that I hold his horse, and I refused. He attempted to horse-whip me, and although he was three years older and larger, I pulled him from his horse and gave him a beating. I thought I'd killed him, so I went home and put a few things together to run away.

"My father came to stand in the door. He asked me about it, and I told him. He said that if I wished to stay he would face them beside me, but I refused. Then he offered me a dozen gold coins, but I knew they were all he had, and I refused that too. Finally we split them, and I shook his hand and left. I never saw him again."

"That was in France?"

"Yes."

"But the name Williams? It doesn't fit."

"It was a name I took when I needed a name in a hurry, that's all."

"What do you think our chances are now with the Kiowas?"

"You can never tell about Indians. They might attack, and they might not. They might try to stampede the herd, and then get us one by one as we try to round them up. This is a war party, hunting trouble. The other tribes who pulled out knew that, and did not want to be involved. If we put on a bold face we might ride right through them."

"I'm going into their camp," Chantry said.

French stared at him. "You're crazy."

"I've heard that an Indian would never kill a man who came willingly into his camp. Maybe before or after, but never in camp unless he is brought in as a prisoner."

"Yes, but you just might find an Indian who didn't think that way."

"In the meantime, you boys can drive the cattle right on . . . by going east."

"I know where Dodge is." Williams threw his cigar into the flames. "If you've got nerve enough you might bring it off, but I wouldn't want to bet on it."

Chantry got to his feet. "I'm turning in." He paused for a moment, and then asked casually, "How much do you trust Rugger?"

"Rugger? He works for me, but I don't trust anybody. Including you."

"You don't have to trust me. You know what I'm doing, and what I'm after."

"What about Rugger? Why do you ask about him?"

"You figure it out. He's your man."

When Tom Chantry stretched out in his bed he looked up at the sky and started to think about what he would do next, but somehow he fell asleep.

The fire crackled, then hissed as a few drops fell. It began to rain quietly and, without waking up, Chantry burrowed deeper into his bedroll.

Chapter 15

The camp was quiet as the men climbed out of their bedrolls in the morning, packed them up, and stowed them in the chuck wagon. The rain had stopped, but the sky was gray and thunder rumbled in the distant hills.

French Williams, Chantry noted, avoided him, as if he regretted having talked so much the previous evening. Chantry took only coffee for breakfast, saddled up, and the herd was moving before the night guard had finished breakfast.

Undoubtedly the Kiowas knew of every move they made, and would be discussing the sudden shift from driving east to pushing the cattle north to the Big Timbers. Sun Chief had told him a good deal about the Indian ways, and it was this that had decided Chantry on riding into the Kiowa camp.

He would wait until almost the last minute so that his ride to the camp would take him only a little time. During that time he would be in danger . . . every yard he gained would be a yard won.

Nobody talked, and the cattle did not seem interested in grazing. They seemed to want to move on, and by now they were well broken to the day's travel, except for a couple of well-known bunch-quitters, and they could be watched.

McKay dropped back beside Chantry. "We're goin' on past the bend of the Clay," he said. "Frenchy says we'll be drivin' sixteen to eighteen miles today."

"The Clay? Does it swing this far east?"

"Uh-huh, an' then it points right north for the Republican."

McKay rode on and the herd moved ahead steadily, occasionally trotting. Obviously Williams was hoping to drive far enough so that he could hit the Big Tim-

bers early in the day. By mid-morning they crossed the
Santa Fe Trail, cut deep with the marks of freighters'
wagons and the countless pack trains that had come
this way.

Once, far ahead on a knoll, they saw two mounted
Indians watching them, but it was not the Kiowas
Chantry was considering today. He drew up, mopping
the sweat from his forehead and watching the cattle go
by. He was thinking of the note left by Rugger and
picked up by the Talrims.

2 Butes . . . Big Timbers . . . Kiwas at Big Timbers
. . . What did it mean? Merely that their next stop was
to be Two Buttes?, and that they were headed for
Big Timbers from there? Or did the message mean
something else? Apparently the Talrims were watching
the herd and would know where it was going. Perhaps
the last phrase was the important one *Kiowas at Big
Timbers*.

Was it a warning? Or was it a suggestion that if anything was to be done it must be done before the Kiowas
could beat them to it?

Did they plan to kill him? Or to steal the herd?

If it was killing they wanted, it would certainly be
best for them to wait and see if the Kiowas would not
do it for them, and if nothing happened at Big Timbers
there was still a chance to do what they wanted, and
even blame the Indians for it.

If it was the herd they wanted, they had best steal
it at once, before the Kiowas could act. But three men
could not take a herd from this crowd unless they had
some others working with them.

Was this a move planned by French Williams himself? Still, he had seemed genuinely puzzled over Chantry's comment on Rugger.

Chantry let the herd move on ahead. He was riding
the blue roan, and if trouble developed its speed would
put him into the action without delay; and by riding
well back he was able to survey the entire herd as well
as the hills around.

Chantry decided he must watch Rugger. If anything
was to happen the man's actions would betray him. He

let his eyes range the hills, and sweep the draws on either side, as much at least as he could see of them.

The country was deceptively open-looking, but there were draws on either side, the beds of intermittent streams, that would make good places of concealment for an ambush.

He suddenly thought of Bone McCarthy. Where was *he?* Had he simply pulled off on his own? Had he been ambushed perhaps to meet the same fate as Paul?

Several times during the morning Chantry saw Rugger and Kincaid meet, confer briefly, and return to their jobs. It was nothing to be remarked . . . it happened a dozen times a day during such long drives, but now his mind was alert with suspicion.

Sun Chief fell back beside him for a short time. The Pawnee had proved a good hand on the drive, working along with the herd in between brief scouting forays into the hills.

Alone on an isolated knob, Chantry stood in his stirrups and let his eyes range the country. The feel of it was coming back—this was the land where he had been a boy, and certainly the place could not have been far from here.

This was a land where a man could grow, where he could build. He found himself wishing he could have known it as the Indians had. He glanced again toward the herd. Rugger and Kincaid were together again.

He was turning his mount to ride back to the drag when he saw the black, muddy trail where a party of riders had gone down the draw to his right. Swinging his horse, he rode down to read sign. There had been perhaps five or six riders, and they must have gone by only minutes before he had reached the crest of the knoll.

Honest men did not avoid a trail drive. They would ride down to pass the time of day, at least. He tried to single out tracks, but he saw no evidence of the Talrims. But all were shod horses, and by the length of their strides they were good stock, running stock.

Tom Chantry skirted the knoll and cut down along the slope, not heading for the drag, but for French

Williams, who was riding point. Williams turned as he approached, no welcome in his eyes.

"Keep your eyes open," Tom said. "We're riding into trouble."

"What's that mean?" French asked.

"I cut sign on half a dozen riders, maybe more. They passed us only a few minutes back and didn't come in to talk."

French Williams rode a few minutes in silence. "So you figure something's building up?"

"You bet I do. I think somebody hopes to grab this herd before we get to Big Timbers."

"That means tonight."

"Or today. Or on the drive tomorrow."

Williams said no more, and rode on. Tom Chantry dropped back, and as he passed Helvie he said again, "Keep your eyes open. We're riding into trouble."

"Kiowas?"

"Maybe somebody closer to home."

Helvie shot him a quick look. "If you mean French, I ride for the brand."

"But who is the brand here? Is it French? Is it me? Or the herd?"

Helvie was silent a moment, considering that. Then he said, "The herd. I'm a cattleman."

"I'll ask nothing more. We both signed on to take this herd all the way."

"McKay will stand."

"I think so too. And I think Dutch will."

Helvie glanced at him. "Dutch? Yes, I think he will. You're not mentioning Rugger or Kincaid."

"No, I'm not. I don't know about them, but they've been doing a lot of getting together this morning." And he told Helvie about the note Rugger had left, and the Talrims picking it up. He also told him about the fresh trail, just over the ridge from the herd. "Maybe I'm chasing wild geese," he said, finally, "but I'm going to ride loose and listen."

Sun Chief hung well back from the drag, urging those steers that lingered behind, but never closing in

tight on the drag. Seeing him there gave Chantry re-
assurance, for he had great respect for the Pawnee and
his awareness of what went on.

But where was McCarthy?

Twice they saw Indians, but they were only watching. If they planned an attack they were content to wait
until the cattle were driven to them.

Were they aware of those other watchers? Chantry
asked Sun Chief. "They know," he answered.

Chantry pulled his horse around the herd and rode
toward the point. He drew up alongside Rugger.
"How're they going?"

"All right." Rugger spoke sullenly, not inviting conversation.

"Keep your eyes open," Chantry said. "We're in Kiowa country."

"I know that."

"There's some outlaws around, too," Chantry added
casually, "but we needn't worry about them. We can
handle them."

Rugger stared at him, narrow-eyed. "Outlaws? There
ain't no outlaws around here."

"What about Bill Coe's outfit from Robber's Roost?
Or the Talrim brothers?"

"They ain't likely to be around," Rugger said.

"No?"

As he turned his horse he smiled at Rugger. What
he had hoped to accomplish was little enough, but he
might have sowed seeds of doubt in Rugger's mind.
At least, he felt that he had worried him, and Rugger
might attempt to call off the impending raid, if that
was what was planned.

But the day passed quietly, and the herd had kept
moving north. It was sundown when they were circled
and bedded down in a small bend of Clay Creek. The
creek was no longer running bank full, but had dropped
to a small stream at the bottom of the creek bed,
enough to water the cattle.

While the others watched over the cattle, Hay Gent
and Chantry rode out to scout the country around. Sun
Chief had already vanished into the gathering dusk.

From the crest of the ridge, a mile back from the camping ground and some two hundred feet higher, they scanned the surrounding territory. There was nothing to be seen.

"Could be an army out there," Gent commented. "There's lots of dips and hollows."

"Sleep light," Chantry advised. "Tonight and tomorrow will be the danger time."

While Rugger and McKay watched the cattle, grazing on the easy slope along the stream, the others ate hurriedly; then Helvie, Hay Gent, and Akin went out while the others came in to eat.

Tom Chantry wasted no time. He ate, drank an extra cup of coffee, and then rolled in his blankets.

The cook had promised to wake him at midnight, but he awoke shortly before that. For a moment he lay perfectly still, listening. He heard no sound . . . not a snore, not the crackle of burning wood . . . nothing.

Suddenly alert, he strained his ears . . . nothing. Very carefully he sat up. The fire was there, burned down to coals now. The wagon was there, the red light from the fire throwing black shadows of its spokes. The bedrolls were there, but all were empty.

He put his hand to his gun . . . but there was no gun.

Slowly, he got to his feet and moved one quick step into the deeper shadow of the brush.

His mouth was dry, his head throbbed dully.

He had been doped . . . *the coffee.*

He stepped back to his bedroll and slid his Winchester from the blankets. That they had been unable to get, for he had been almost lying on it. Holding it in one hand, he picked up his boots with the other, and stepped back into the shadows. Putting down the rifle, he pulled on his boots, shrugged into a coat, and then took up his hat and rifle.

He edged around the fire and started toward the remuda. It was gone . . . all the horses gone.

He stood for a minute trying to clear his dulled mind . . . he had suspected an attempt to stampede the herd, and he had tied the line-back dun out in the brush, saddled and ready.

Now he slipped back there like a ghost . . . the dun was there, a good fifty yards back in the brush along the route by which they had come.

He tightened the cinch and stepped into the saddle, coiling the picket rope as he sat there, thinking.

Then he rode out to the cattle. And they were there, bedded down and quiet; but no, riders rode around them, no voices sang.

Oddly, at that moment he remembered his own curiosity about why cowpunchers sang to cattle. The answer was simple enough. The longhorn steer is a wild animal, quick to stampede, and the men riding herd at night sang so that the cattle would not be surprised at the sound of their approach. Hearing the familiar voices reassured the animals, and they continued to doze or sleep. Trail drivers sang during the night watch more for the sake of the cattle than for their own amusement.

Riding up to them now, he began to sing softly, just loud enough so they could hear him. Slowly he swung around the herd, then made a second circle, farther out. He was looking for anybody or anything he might find. But he found nothing.

What had happened? Had they abandoned him, and the cattle? Had they all been spirited away by Indians? If so, why had he been left? Was this part of Williams' game to win the herd? And what could he do now? What could he do alone?

As dawn began to break he rode back to the camp. He found no signs of struggle. The bedrolls lay as they had been left. Evidently the men had got up, pulled on their boots, and walked quietly away, whether of their own volition or under the threat of a gun he had no way of knowing.

Going to the chuck wagon he dug out a side of bacon, filled a small sack with coffee, a couple of loaves of bread, and some odds and ends. He took a spare coffeepot, his cup, and whatever else he might need. Then he rode back to the herd.

The cattle were already up and stretching, grazing a little. The brindle steer that had been the leader since the third day had moved out and, head up, was waiting.

"All right, boy, let's go!" Chantry said, and he started off, riding point. The brindle steer followed. Slowly, the others fell in behind, broken to the trail by long days of driving.

How long he could keep them together he did not know. The brindle steer pointed north toward the Big Timbers, and Tom Chantry circled back, driving in the laggards. The herd was moving.

Warily, he rode back to the point, watching the country around, which was relatively open.

What had he been expected to do? Cut and run? Start scouting for them and leave the cattle? Left to themselves, the herd would soon scatter, and no doubt they would soon realize he was alone and begin to fall out of the drive anyway. All he had going for him was that brindle steer and the ingrained habit of the days on the trail. But for the time the cattle moved off willingly enough.

The cattle had been moving steadily for nearly an hour when the Indians appeared.

First there was one, then another, then a dozen. They lined the crest of the low rise half a mile on his left and watched him.

They could see he was alone, one man and a great herd of cattle, held together only by the habit of the trail.

Suddenly from out of a draw, Sun Chief appeared. He rode to the drag, bunching those cattle that were beginning to lag and scatter.

A moment later, Bone McCarthy came from the shadow of a juniper on a low ridge, and rode down to the flank, and the cattle moved on toward Big Timbers and the Arkansas River.

At noon the Indians were still with them, watching. Bone circled around and turned the point inward, and between them they bunched the cattle. With Sun Chief and Chantry standing guard, Bone McCarthy fried some bacon and made coffee.

"I found your railhead," Bone told him. "It's this side of the Colorado line, coming on about a mile a day, more or less. I found something else, too. I found a telegram for you."

He handed the hand-written message to Chantry. It was brief and to the point.

> *Reverses here. Without the herd I have nothing. All depends on you. Doris sends love.*
> *Earnshaw.*

"Did you read this?"

"Couldn't help it, open like that. Besides, I figured if I lost it I'd still know what it had to say. . . . Tough."

"He's a good man, Bone. I can't let him down."

"Three men? More than two thousand head of stock, no remuda, and those Kiowas lookin' down our necks? Man, you've bought yourself a big job."

Chantry glanced toward the ridge. The Kiowas were there, watching, and somewhere nearby he could be sure the outlaws who wanted his cattle were watching too.

But most of all, he thought of French Williams. No matter what the man had been, Chantry had always, deep down within himself, believed that French would play his hand out, fair and square.

They rode out to the cattle and Sun Chief came to the fire.

The Kiowas were still out there, more of them now, and the Big Timbers were not far ahead, where he had promised to visit the Wolf Walker.

"Boss?" McCarthy said.

"What?"

"We got company."

Chantry turned in the direction McCarthy indicated.

A rider was coming toward them, walking his horse, and singing *Tenting Tonight On the Old Camp Ground*.

It was Mobile Callahan.

Chapter 16

"Looks to me, Chantry, like you could use a good hand," Callahan said. "I've been round and about, and up the trail a time or two, and I'm a fair hand with a rope or a gun."

"You've got a job."

"Don't want you should worry about that. Mr. Sparrow is payin' me plenty to help you get to the railhead."

"Sparrow? *Paying* you?"

"Uh-huh. He some kin o' yours?"

"No."

Mobile glanced toward the Indians. "You've got to figure on them, of course, but what you really need are horses. What happened?"

Chantry explained in as few words as possible, his eyes straying from the cattle to the Indians.

"You think it was French Williams?"

Chantry shrugged. "The Talrims are around, and I think Rugger was planning something with somebody else. All I know is that everything I've got is riding with this herd; and worse yet, everything my boss has got is, too. If we can bring it in we can make something; and if not, a good man and his daughter have gone down with us."

They rode on in silence, keeping moving constantly, but trying to save their horses as much as possible.

At intervals all four men got off and walked. By noon they could see the trees along the Arkansas, the looming tops of the Big Timbers. They circled the herd, and while the cattle were resting they built a fire.

"I'm going on into the Indian camp," Chantry told them. "I said I was going, and I must. I don't know what they are planning, but my chances are as good there as here. Stay with the herd, but if you're at-

tacked, scatter and run for it. We can always get together and fight again. I don't want to lose any of you."

"If you go into that camp," McCarthy warned,
"you'll lose your hair."

"Maybe." He hesitated, finishing his coffee. "On the
other hand, I might make a deal for some horses. You
can help me cut out about six head of good beef. I'll
drive them in for a gift to Wolf Walker."

From the knolls the Indians watched as the men cut
out the beef, and they followed Chantry when he
started for the Big Timbers with them.

Suddenly, four Indians came riding down to him.
They drew up.

"I am going to your camp," Chantry said, speaking
slowly. "I take a present to Wolf Walker. To He-Who-
Walks-With-Wolves."

One older buck with a strong profile demanded,
"Why you do this?"

"I am Tom Chantry. The Wolf Walker and I fought.
It was a good fight. He fought with great strength. It
is good that we be friends."

Nothing more was said, but the Kiowas closed in
around him and around the cattle. Soon they dipped
down, forded the river as far as an island, then went on
to the further bank and were among the cottonwoods.

The huge trees were scattered, and the grass was
thick beneath them. There was much shade, and the
small fallen branches and twigs provided kindling for
fires. Here and there were dead trees, and he could see
where some had been felled in the past.

Suddenly the lodges were before him. This was the
sort of camp the Kiowas or Comanches preferred,
among open timber. The Sioux liked their camps near
water, but away from timber because of their dread of
ambush. The Osage, Omahas, and Shawnees preferred
dense thickets.

As they rode in, women and children came from the
lodges, from among the trees, and from the banks of
the streams. Several warriors strode up to Chantry and
one grasped his bridle with a strong hand.

"I come to make talk with the Wolf Walker," he
said.

An Indian pushed back the flap of his tipi and stood up. It was the Wolf Walker.

"I bring you a gift," Tom Chantry said, and he gestured toward the cattle. "We fought well, you and I." He held out his hand. "I am Tom Chantry."

An older Indian who stood nearby grunted and said something to those who stood about him.

Wolf Walker said, "Red Buffalo speaks your name. But he speak Bor-den."

"Borden Chantry was my father." Suddenly Tom remembered the Indians who had come often to the ranch when the weather was cold and hunting was bad. His father had fed them, had traded horses with them.

"The Kiowas were our good friends," he said. "They came often to my father's lodge. I was papoose."

The old Indian grunted. "Come! Eat!"

Chantry dismounted and followed the older Indian to his lodge. Others followed them, and they sat cross-legged on the floor.

"Where you go?" the old Indian presently demanded.

"To the Wagon-That-Smokes," Chantry said, "to ship the cattle to my people who are hungry."

"You men . . . where they go?"

He shrugged. "Some friends, some no friends to me. They steal my horses. They wish to steal cattle . . . the wo-haws," he added, remembering the Indian name for oxen.

As he ate with them, they asked of his father. "He is dead," he said. "Three men killed him—long ago."

"You kill them now?"

"I have lost their sign. Many years I was far away." He gestured toward the east. "They are gone. Maybe dead."

"No dead," the old Indian said quietly. "Me know them. Two men are where iron trail ends."

"What!" he exclaimed. He was not sure they had understood, or that he had. "You say the men who killed my father are at the railhead?"

"I say. Five men now. Three big men"—he indicated the rusty stain on a pot—"hair like so. He tapped the rusty spot. "One who has no scalp, one the Little Bird."

It made no sense, but he was not interested now in the men who had killed his father; that was all water under the bridge. Nor did he believe he would find them at the railhead. All he wanted now was freedom from attack, and he believed he had won that.

Any man who entered an Indian village of his own volition was safe as long as he remained there. Though anyone outside the tribe was a potential enemy, peace within the village was of first importance. As there had been no chance of outrunning the Kiowas with a trail herd, his best chance had been to come among them. Without a doubt they believed he had returned to avenge his father; had he denied it they would have lost respect for him, and any friendship they might have had would be gone.

Until now he had almost forgotten that his father had been a friend of the Kiowas, one of the fiercest of all the Plains tribes. He had traded with them, fed them when they were hungry, sheltered them often, and interceded for them with the Army. He had done it out of respect and admiration, not in fear, and this the Indians knew. It followed that they would have known who killed him.

He got to his feet. "I will come again to your village," he said. "My father was your friend, and so shall I be."

He turned to Wolf Walker and thrust out his hand. "Someday we will hunt together."

The Indian took his hand, and the black eyes gleamed.

Turning his back, Chantry went out, and an Indian boy held his horse. He stepped into the saddle, raised his right hand, and rode away.

When he got back to the herd the cattle were moving. The riders came back and gathered around him —Callahan, Sun Chief, and McCarthy. "What happened?" Mobile asked.

He explained, and then added, "They told me the men who killed my father are at the railhead."

"Waitin' for you?" Mobile asked.

"After all these years? Why?"

"When you've lived a few years longer you'll no longer wonder at the motives of men. They're mixed, Mr. Chantry. And sometimes they don't know the why of them, themselves." After a moment, he went on. "Sometimes a man regrets. You ever know regret, Mr. Chantry? I have. It is a powerful motive, a mighty powerful one with some folks."

"And maybe they think you've come back to hunt them down," McCarthy commented ironically. "Maybe they just figure to get you before you get them."

After a moment Mobile Callahan said, "Did you see them? Would you know them now?"

He considered that a moment. "I don't know. One of them was slight, and young. The other two—well, one of them was very big, and red-headed. But I doubt if I would know them now. It has been a long time."

"Being gun-handy is a risky thing, Mr. Chantry," Callahan said. "If a gun comes easy to your hand you're apt to let it happen when it shouldn't. I've used a gun a time or two, and most times whoever was on the other end had it a-comin', but there was a time—"

He swung wide and brought a laggard steer back to the herd.

"There was a time when I killed a man that didn't need killin'. It was in a poker game. Nobody blamed me for the shootin', but it didn't do me a damn bit o' good to tell myself that I gave him ever' chance—I knew I hadn't. The gun came too easy to my hand.

"He had a wife and three kids, and he said her name when he was dyin'. . . .

"I did what I could for 'em."

Mobile Callahan was silent for a few minutes. "I regret that shootin', Mr. Chantry, I surely do. I always have."

Tom Chantry rode out to the point, thinking about what had happened. Where were French Williams and the others? Had they deserted him, or had they been taken away at gun point? Had he been doped that night, in the coffee?

By sundown they were nine miles west. Whoever had told him there were only three days of driving to go had been mistaken. Of course, there had been delays. There had been frequent stops, some of them overlong, and their route had not always been the most direct.

How far now? He wanted to ask Bone McCarthy or Sun Chief, but they were scattered out and there was no chance. The herd had handled easily so far, but it seemed as if they were becoming aware that the riders were fewer. However, the old brindle steer stayed right on the line where his nose was pointed, heading toward the railroad as if he could smell the steam and the cinders.

The sun was low and it was time to circle for the night when the riders came upon them. A moment before they had been moving placidly enough, and then, almost out of nowhere, or out of the sinking sun, the charging horsemen, the thunder of guns, and the longhorns broke into a run.

Mobile Callahan was riding drag, Sun Chief was working the north side of the herd, and Bone McCarthy was on the south. Chantry himself was riding point, and when the herd broke he was swept along, riding at breakneck speed to keep from being trampled by the frightened, maddened cattle.

Somebody yelled, "Kill him! Kill Chantry!"

As the dust and the cattle closed around him he saw one person, sitting a horse alone on a small knoll, watching him. It was Sarah.

And then his world was filled with the thunder of hoofs, the shouts of men, the shots—and somewhere a scream of pain drowned by the roar of the stampede.

Chapter 17

There was no fighting the maddened rush of more than two thousand head of cattle. The sudden charge from out of the sun, the burst of firing, and the cattle were gone. His only hope was to run, to keep ahead of them, and to pray that his horse would keep its feet. If the horse fell . . .

He was surrounded by tossing horns, and there seemed no chance to break out of the herd. There was nothing to do but run with them until the impetus of the charge was broken and the cattle stopped of their own volition.

Suddenly the sun was gone, but the red glow remained in the sky. He had his six-shooter out, ready to kill a steer to pile them up if he could, but so far the dun was keeping its feet and was running freely. He had no idea how far they had run, but he knew that his horse could not hold such a pace for long.

A gap showed between the steer ahead and the steer to the right, and Chantry put the dun over, hoping he might work his way free of the herd. Even in this moment of danger the thought came to him: who had screamed back there? The stampede must have caught somebody and trampled him down.

Then he found another gap, eased into it, and suddenly he was at the edge of the herd and was fighting his way free of it. He had run another half-mile before he was out of the press of cattle and running the flank.

He slowed the dun, watching the herd stream by. The time was not right for turning it, and anyway he did not have the man power. His best bet was to let them run, then as they slowed down, begin gradually turning them to point them north once more.

The stars were out; the sky was black above, the

earth was black below. The cattle were slowing now, the fever run out of them, and the fear gone.

He listened, and above the steady pound of hoofs he heard only the occasional clack of horns bashing together. No voices, no other sound.

He moved in close to the herd now, and began to sing to them, trying to calm them, and pushing a little toward the east as he did so. Slowly, the cattle turned before him. He saw a few scattered ones, and swung wide to intercept them, turning them back into the herd.

As he had them streaming out toward the east, suddenly three riders topped out on a knoll. Instantly he recognized one of them—it was Sarah!

And the Talrims!

At the same instant a shot rang out from behind him, he felt a solid blow on the cantle of his saddle, and heard a bullet whine off into the distance. He managed one quick glance over his shoulder and saw four riders closing in from behind. Sarah and the Talrims all threw up their rifles at once, and he slapped spurs to his horse.

The dun was running its heart out now. It went over the hill and down a ridge, and Chantry saw ahead of him several tall cottonwoods. He almost pulled up.

Though the trees were a good mile off, he saw in the scene something more, something familiar.

It was home! The home ranch!

A bullet kicked dust just head of him, and he threw one wild glance over his shoulder. Fanned out behind him were seven or eight riders. Another was closing in from the flank.

A volley came from behind, and he felt the dun stumble. He raced into the trees, swung around and pulled up, staring at his old home.

Only the shell remained. The roof had partly fallen in, some of the logs had been pulled from the end wall to build a fire. The old barn where he had once played was gone; there were only the charred remains.

He heard the pound of hoofs and swung his horse around. There was no place here to make a stand. He could only run until—

The Hole . . . it rushed into his mind.

He had not thought of The Hole in years. Was it still there? Was it large enough to take a man? He shucked his rifle from the scabbard and rode the staggering dun down the draw, then kicked free of the saddle, and dropped. As he did so, he grabbed at the saddlebags and had barely got them when the dun slid to a stand, half falling.

"Sorry, old boy, I can't help you now!" He ducked and ran.

He saw the brush where he had played at Indian as a child; the ditch cut by runoff water was larger now. He ran along it, safely hidden now, as he had been then. He went over the slight rise and into a buffalo wallow. The wind had scoured it deeper; he crawled, slid, and worked his way ahead.

He could hear them yelling and swearing as they searched around the ruins of the old house. He went over the narrow ridge and saw the spot before him.

The sound of hoofs was not far off, and he heard an angry shout. "His horse is down! We got him!"

He ran up to the place. No water. No spring any longer . . . only a sandy basin about a dozen feet across and a slab of rock where the hole should have been.

He grabbed the rock with both hands and stood it on edge. There was a hole there, scarcely large enough for a man—but it was a hole.

Was it deep enough? His only chance was to try. He turned around and backed into it, kicking obstructions away. When he got in all the way he pulled his Winchester in after him.

He found a ledge on which to place the rifle, then reaching out he grasped the slab. At first it refused to budge. He dug at its base and it slid forward, falling over the opening, closing him in. . . .

He was buried alive.

Literally, he was buried. Could he push the stone outward again? Could he dig around it? As he remembered, there had been a solid ledge there.

Crouching in the hole, he waited. Had he left any marks they could see? The sand of the basin had been churned by the feet of buffalo or cattle. But if the stone had left any fresh earth exposed—what then?

What was most in his favor was the sheer unlikelihood of a cave or opening anywhere around. There was simply no probability of such a thing.

As he crouched there he heard horses' hoofs again, and muffled talk, then a woman's voice. It was shrill, and he could make out the words faintly. "Nobody can vanish into nothing like that! He's got to be here!"

For a little while the muttered talk continued, then there was silence. He put a hand on his rifle and moved it about. Behind the ledge where it had been lying was a solid wall, but behind him and on the other side of him, he touched nothing.

He listened, but there was now no sound outside. The air around him seemed fresh enough. He felt in his pocket and found a match, and struck it on the hammer of his rifle. The match flared, burned up brightly, and he peered around.

The cave sloped down toward the back. Where he had crawled in, it was a narrow tunnel, no more than three feet across, and where he now stood it was a little more than six feet. Behind him, he had the impression of vastness, and from somewhere he heard the drip of water.

When he had found this cave as a child he had shown it to his father, but there had never been time to explore it. How large it was or where it led he had no idea.

From a few sticks, perhaps pulled in by some animal long ago, he selected a couple and lighted them. They were dry, and they burned well enough. He made his way down the slope and found himself in a fairly large room from which a passage led. At the bottom there was a pool of clear water. A small stream trickled into it, and this at one time must have been the spring he had drunk from as a boy, but the floor of the cave seemed to have fallen and the trickle of water no longer reached the surface at this point.

He tasted the water and found that it was cold and fresh. He drank, then drank again. Then he returned to the spot near the opening and sat in the dark and chewed on a piece of jerky. When it was finished, he crawled up in the hole and pushed against the slab of stone. It would not budge.

He pushed again, but it did not move. Desperately, he lunged against it, but in the narrow passage it was difficult to exert any great force. Finally he drew back, struggling for breath.

He sat down and fought against the panic that was welling up within him. He forced himself to think, remembering something his father had said. "Use your head, boy. That head of yours is the one thing that makes you different from an animal of any other kind. When you feel yourself getting scared, sit down, relax, and let yourself be calm. Then study it out. You will find an answer."

He sat quietly, and slowly the panic left him. That stone weighed no more than fifty or sixty pounds. It was several inches thick and it had slid down from above the hole. The old runoff water from the spring had fallen into the sandy basin, several inches lower than the hole. So if he put the pressure on the very top of the slab, it might be tipped forward and over.

But what if those outside had found what he had done? Suppose they knew there was a hole here and that he had crawled in? And knowing that, suppose they had heaped earth over the rock, packed it in, to let him stay there and die?

There was no use in supposing. He was not going to escape his dilemma by sitting and worrying about it. What he had to do was try for a way out.

He crawled up in the narrow hole once more, but this time he did not fight the rock. He felt with his fingers for the very top of the slab, and then he pushed.

Nothing happened.

He waited a moment, gathered strength, and pushed harder; the slab moved and a trickle of sand fell into the cave from above.

A moment longer he waited, and then he pushed again. The slab moved outward a little more and fell, and the hole gaped at the top, letting in both light and air.

Again he pushed . . . and a bullet clipped the top of the slab and spat sand into his face.

"Stay there!" The unfamiliar voice was harsh. "You're dead, so stay dead!"

He backed away. He might chance a shot, but he would have to get far enough into the hole to be able to see a target outside before he could fire. On the other hand, they would have a target they could not easily miss.

He put his rifle down carefully, felt for the sticks, and held a match to the frayed end of one. It caught, went out, but caught with the next match. Taking up his rifle and several other sticks, he went down the slope toward the back. The flame bent slightly back toward the way he had come. There was a draft here, a slight movement of air from somewhere ahead.

He went on, moving as swiftly as he could. He found occasional small pieces of wood, changed sticks, lighting from his previous torch. He crossed the roomlike area and glimpsed several dark openings, but went on in the direction of the draft.

There was a trickle of water on the cave floor, and he bent over and dampened his face. It cooled quickly from the movement of air. He had walked perhaps a hundred steps when he saw a faint gleam of light. He lighted another dry stick and hurried on.

The gleam of light came from a small opening only a few yards ahead, but suddenly he came to an abrupt halt. For the light he saw was coming from an opening at the edge of a heavy canvas curtain, weighted at the bottom with a wooden pole. He went up to it and pulled it slightly aside.

He looked around in amazement, then swore softly. He was standing at the back of the root cellar on the ranch where he had grown up. Before him was a wall of shelves. He started to move it, and found the wall turned on a pivot.

The place was empty, dusty, long-undisturbed by anything other than pack rats. Here his family had stored vegetables they had raised in their small kitchen garden, and here, his father had always warned them, they were to take shelter in case of Indian attack.

He remembered the day he had shown his father his cave that he called The Hole. His father had been properly astonished, properly admiring; and his father, he now knew, had known of it all the time.

Now he knew where he was, and he knew where the ones outside must be. He checked his rifle and went to the door. It was half hidden behind the bole of a huge old cottonwood, and there was a little light coming through the crack where the boards of the door had shrunk. He peered out and could see nothing, but he did hear horses cropping grass.

Rifle in his right hand, ready to fire, he moved the door with his left. Dust and sand fell, but it moved easily.

Nothing out there but the trees and grass, the ruins of the barn, some scattered gray boards, and the brush beyond. Then to the right he glimpsed the horses, cropping the grass.

He went up the last step, and moved out. He stood listening, but heard nothing.

From behind the cottonwood he scouted the area carefully with eyes and ears. Nothing.

He walked toward the horses, and took the bridle of the first one. He stepped into the saddle, and catching the bridle of the other, walked the horse carefully away. The men who watched the hole for him could continue to watch, but they would have a long wait.

He rode to where he had left the dun. The horse was down, and dead. He swore bitterly. The dun had been a good horse, a noble horse, and he wanted to see no horse die. He stepped down, stripped his gear from the dead animal, and exchanged it for that on the horse he was riding. Then he mounted up.

Leading the spare horse, he started north. The first thing to do was to find the herd.

Chapter 18

From the hill above Butte Springs he glimpsed some scattered cattle and rode toward them. He gathered them, taking it easy to save his horses; he led the extra mount so he could switch if need be. There were eighteen head, and he bunched them, then pushed on, gathering more.

Beyond Plum Creek he could see still others scattered out and grazing. The day was warm and clear and his eyes ranged the country around, alert to sight any movement of men or animals. If he could gather enough of the herd he would start them toward the railroad, which must be north of him now, and near the river. He would drive what cattle he could gather, pick up some hands, and return to make a sweep of the plains.

Beyond Granada Creek he could see the dusty trace that marked the Sante Fe Trail. By the time he was midway between Plum and Granada he had gathered more than a hundred head. Leaving them to graze, he trailed the reins of the horse he was riding and switched to the other. He left his first mount with the cattle, rode west, and began to gather more.

Alternating horses he had by nightfall added another two hundred head to his herd, finding them often in bunches of a dozen or more. He pushed them north a couple of miles to fresh grass, and when they had begun to lie down, he made his own camp near a pool of water left from the recent rains in an arroyo that emptied into Plum Creek. He did not build a fire.

With his horses picketed close by, he went to sleep, trusting to them to alert him to any danger. The night passed quietly, and before dawn he was up, saddled his horses, and rode out to continue his gather.

A few cattle had drifted into the basin and he added

them to what he had, then crossed the Sante Fe Trail into the breaks around the head of Wolf Creek. On the slope below him he saw some five hundred head of cattle bunched together, and two picketed horses. Keeping out of sight, he worked around on foot until he could see their camp.

Two men were sleeping under a bank near some junipers. A thin tendril of smoke lifted from the remains of their fire. Recovering his horse, he rode in a small circle to a place among the junipers near them, and then crept down the slope until he was on the bank just above them.

A dim path, evidently made by buffalo or antelope, went around the junipers and down into their camp. It was all he needed. Moving quietly, he made his way closer until he stood in their camp. Actually, his movements were practically silent.

He picked up their rifles and put them behind him, then went to the sleeping men, each of whom had a six-shooter near him. As he bent over, holding his rifle in his right hand, and just about to reach with his left and pick up the nearest man's gun belt, the man lunged up from his bed and grabbed at the rifle. As he lunged, Tom Chantry swung a short butt-stroke to the temple and the man dropped as though hit with an axe.

Coolly, Chantry picked up the other gun belt, then booted the sleeping man in the ribs.

He raised his head and said, "What the hell?" And then he saw Chantry standing over him.

"Get up," Chantry said. "And get your boots on. We've got some cattle to drive."

"Go to hell!"

Chantry stooped suddenly, grabbed the man's bed and jerked. As he tumbled from the blankets, Chantry stepped in and kicked him in the stomach.

The man rolled over, retching.

"Now get up and get your boots on," Chantry repeated. "You're going to find out what it means to steal another man's cattle."

The rustler gasped for a few minutes. He looked at his companion. "What happened to *him?*"

"He got a little ambitious. Maybe his skull is busted."

"An' you don't give a damn?"

"No, I don't. What happens to a thief is his own tough luck. When you start out to steal, you're anybody's game, remember that. . . . Now you get your horse saddled. We're driving these cattle."

"What about him?"

"If he revives, he can help you. If he doesn't, the buzzards will take care of him. Get moving."

Chantry backed to the fire and picked up the coffeepot. Some coffee sloshed in it, and he drank from the edge. Keeping a good distance, he let his eyes range the area, seeking out any possible cover.

A groan from the other man alerted him, and he saw him stirring. He walked over and booted him. "Get up! Get into your boots."

"I'll kill you for this!" the man growled.

"Get into the saddle," Chantry said. "If you drive those cattle and don't get funny, I may let you live. Make a wrong move and I'll shoot you. I'm out of patience."

With the two rustlers working under his rifle, Chantry gathered the bunch they had and drove them over to his own small herd, which had scattered a bit as they grazed.

When the cattle were bunched with his own, he faced the two rustlers, staying fifty yards off from them. His rifle on them, he said, "What became of my riders?"

"Wouldn't you like to know?" said the heavier of the two with a sneer.

"Yes, I would." Tom Chantry smiled pleasantly at them. "You boys can tell me or not, as you choose. I've got this rifle, and I can drop a running rabbit with it, and you boys make a good deal bigger target. You're cow thieves—maybe murderers. Whether you get out of this alive depends on how you cooperate, and on my whim. I've a good notion to shoot you both where you stand. If you're found dead out here nobody is going to ask questions. Of course, it would make it easier to handle the cattle if you boys work along and help."

They looked at him, and they did not like what they saw. The rifle was ready, and they judged him as they would themselves. After all, why should he keep them alive?

"All right," the bigger man agreed. "We'll ride along and he'p with the cattle. An' we'll stay right with you up to the rails. But what then?"

Chantry shrugged. "I don't want either of you. You help me get my cattle to the railhead, and then you can get out of the country as fast as you can ride. Start any sooner than within sight of the rails, and I'll shoot you, wherever it is."

Would he? At that moment Chantry had no idea. He knew that, come what might, he must get these cattle to the railroad.

He strapped their rifles to his own saddle, and their gun belts as well. They started the cattle, pointing them north. It could not be more than twenty miles to the railroad now, and probably was less.

For an hour they moved steadily. Chantry worked well back, out of the dust, his rifle ready to use at any sign of betrayal.

But they had no need for betrayal. For suddenly, without warning, a dozen riders appeared. They swept down upon him, four of them rushing at the herd, the others forming up near him, a few yards off. And they came at a time when his rifle was in his scabbard, the first time all morning when that had been the case.

Rugger was there, and Kincaid. Koch was there, grinning at him, a triumphant grin. The others were strangers. To his relief, not one of the men with whom he had worked so well, McKay, Hay Gent, or Helvie, was among them.

"Looks like you he'ped us round 'em up," Rugger said, "an' we thank you for that. Now we're takin' them over."

They were going to kill him. Koch would never have it otherwise, nor Rugger either, for that matter.

"Let me make you an offer, boys," Chantry said pleasantly, and drew his gun.

They were off guard, his speed was greater than they expected, and their reaction time was against them. He drew, and shot Rugger out of the saddle, then switched the gun to Koch.

Koch's rifle was coming up and Chantry's bullet, aimed for his mid-section, hit the hammer and glanced upward, catching Koch under the chin. He toppled from his horse, blood streaming from his throat, and the horse went galloping away over the prairie.

Rugger was on the ground; Koch was gone. The others found themselves staring at a six-shooter that seemed to have come from nowhere.

"Shuck those guns!" Tom Chantry said. "Or I'll empty some saddles! Quick!"

Kincaid hesitated, and a bullet broke his arm at the elbow.

Reaching over to one of the captured holsters, Chantry took another six-shooter with his left hand.

There was no need for it. The others were loosening their gun belts. The shooting had happened so fast that not one of them had even had time to register the need for a draw.

"Now get out of here!"

With a thunder of hoofs, the riders were streaking away. The men near him swung their horses and started to ride away, and he let them go.

Once more he was alone with the cattle . . . and then he saw why the others had fled. Riding toward him in a long array, was a line of at least fifty Kiowa braves.

Ahead of them they were driving several hundred head of cattle.

Wolf Walker rode toward him, a dozen braves close behind. He stopped in a swirl of dust.

"We come. We help. We drive wo-haws for friend."

"I thank you," Chantry said.

Slowly the herd bunched again. From somewhere came Old Brindle and stepped into the lead, and the cattle moved off slowly. From out of the draws other bunches of cattle came, driven by Kiowas. By nightfall the cattle all seemed to have been gathered.

But Tom Chantry was worried. Where were French Williams and the others? Williams himself was an uncertain quantity, a man he had never trusted completely. Helvie, McKay, Gent, and Akin had all seemed good men, and dependable.

Behind it all, he was sure, were the operations of

Sarah. She must have found and employed the Talrim brothers, and she must have recruited the others to help her . . . she would know what arguments to use. If what she wanted was ownership of the cattle, she would have clear title once he and Williams were out of the way.

But now there seemed no way she could win. The railroad was only a few miles away, and the Kiowas who guarded the cattle were fighting men, not to be trifled with. Chantry recalled what she had told Paul about not paying the men who helped her, and he was sure she had something of the sort in mind now.

She was not the sort to give up easily, but what could she do?

She must believe that the cards were all in her hands. She probably had French Williams a prisoner, or had killed him. And perhaps she still thought that Tom Chantry was trapped in The Hole.

Some of the outlaws who had been driving the cattle might have gotten in touch with her, but that he doubted.

What would she do now?

The cattle would be delivered at the railhead, placed aboard cars there, and shipped east. It began to look as if Sarah was whipped, and French Williams, too.

And then he remembered that at the railhead were the men who had killed his father. What was he going to do about that? And what did they plan to do?

Chapter 19

The river was not far off now, and the railroad followed it. He pointed the way, occasionally glancing back to see if any enemies were in sight, but he trusted the Indians to alert him to any danger. This was the short-grass country, blue grama, buffalo grass, and some needle grasses. Patches of prickly pear appeared now and again, and yucca, often called soap weed from the Indians' use of it, dotted the plains.

The cattle, seeming to sense the river with its abundance of water, moved steadily onward, and the Kiowas proved efficient herdsmen, working with the cattle as if born to it. They were magnificent horsemen and managed their quick ponies without effort.

Twice Chantry glimpsed antelope, and once a small bunch of buffalo, moving southward, away from the river. Suddenly, from far off, he heard a train whistle.

The Kiowas drew up to listen, and even the steers lifted their heads, staring wild-eyed, at the unfamiliar sound. A thin trail of smoke showed in the sky.

They topped out on a low rise and the river lay before them, and somewhat to the east of north, they saw a cluster of buildings and a train, its locomotive giving off the smoke he had seen.

There was a sudden flurry of action near the town, men running, and mounted men beginning to assemble.

Wolf Walker came up to Chantry. "They see us," he said grimly. "Think we come for fight."

"Hold them. I'll ride ahead."

He started down the slight slope at a canter to meet the horsemen. He was nearly at the town when he came up to them, two dozen men armed and ready to fight.

"Take it easy, gentlemen!" he said. "Those Kiowas are driving my cattle for me."

"Like hell!" blustered a huge bearded man. "This here's a squaw man—he's one of them!"

"I'm not one of them, and I am driving these cattle from Cimarron to load on the steam cars. Rustlers scattered my herd and the Kiowas helped me gather them and drive them on. They have been very helpful."

"I don't believe that!" the big man exclaimed. "I—"

Chantry swung his horse to face him. "My friend," he said, "I am losing patience with you. If you say that again you'd better have a gun in your hand."

The man started to speak, then stopped, but his eyes were ugly.

"Hold your horses, Butler," another man said. "Sparrow told me about this man. He's the one that stock buyer is waitin' for. This here's Tom Chantry."

"Chantry!" Suddenly Butler was all confidence. "You're the one that took water from Dutch Akin! Well, by—!"

"Mr. Butler," Chantry interrupted, "you are right. I am the man who refused to fight a stranger against whom I had no animosity. Under the same circumstances I would do the same thing again.

"However, a few miles back along the trail you will find two men who attempted to take my cattle, Rugger and Koch. You will find them dead. I'm afraid their intentions caused me to develop some animosity very quickly, and you are now creating the same situation. If I were you I'd throttle down while you are still in a condition to do so."

He turned to the other man. "Thank you, sir, for speaking up. I need a few good hands to take my herd and bring it in. The Kiowas would prefer not to come into town."

"I'll help." The man turned in his saddle. "Joe? How about you, Bob and Sam? Want to help this man?"

Chantry rode back with them and cut out a dozen steers. "Take them," he told the Kiowas, "but wait until I return." And he rode on to the town.

There was little enough there—a dozen flimsy shacks, two dozen sprawling tents. Saloons, dance halls, general stores, a barber shop, horse dealers, stock buyers, and two hotel tents, as well as the private cars on sidings.

Chantry swung down in front of the big tent with a General Store sign and went inside. He said, "I want twenty blankets, twenty new hunting knives, and twenty packets of tobacco."

"You a trader?"

"No," he replied, "just a man paying off a debt."

A voice spoke behind him. "There are other kinds of debts. They all have to be paid." It was Sparrow.

"I have met your Mr. Earnshaw. A fine gentleman, and a lovely daughter." Sparrow studied him thoughtfully. "Mr. Chantry, I understand you and Miss Earnshaw are to be married?"

"We have discussed it."

"Fine . . . fine. I am glad to hear it. And then you will be going back east?"

Chantry hesitated. *Was* he? "I don't know," he said. "Temporarily, perhaps."

"If you stay here there will be problems."

"Why not? There are problems everywhere."

"These are different. I understand you killed two men on the trail?"

"It was necessary. I did not wish to do it."

Sparrow was quiet for a moment, and then he said, "Have you heard that the men who killed your father are here, in this town?"

"I heard it."

"You intend to do nothing about it?"

"That was long ago, Mr. Sparrow. I believe that circumstances will make them pay far better than I could. If they leave me alone, I'll not disturb them."

"You are right, I think," Sparrow said, "in saying that circumstances can make them pay. For one reason or another, all of them have suffered."

"You know them?"

"Yes."

Chantry turned abruptly. "I must ride back to the Indians. These are presents to pay them in some measure for what they have done. These things will be useful to them."

"You amaze me, Mr. Chantry. Only a few weeks in

this country, and the Kiowas, one of the bloodiest
tribes on the plains, come to your assistance."

"It was because of my father. Long ago when I was
only a boy we lived out here. The Kiowas were always
welcome on our ranch, and during bad times we fed
them, although I suspect we could little afford it. We
never had much, you know. And just when my father
had built a herd that could make him wealthy, he was
wiped out by a norther."

Sparrow was silent. After a moment he said, "Your
father was a good man. Those men who killed him little
knew what kind of man he was, and they must not
kill you."

Chantry smiled. "They won't. I'm quite good with a
gun, you know."

Sparrow's eyes were bleak. "Yes, I was afraid of that.
You have your father's hands and his eyes." He put a
hand on Chantry's sleeve. It was a sudden, uncharacter-
istic gesture, and it startled Chantry.

"Please. Don't carry it any further, Tom. Don't kill
anyone else. A man can go too far with it."

"Thanks," was Tom Chantry's only reply.

On a high rise, with the sun growing lower in the
sky, he presented his gifts to the Kiowas.

"You have helped me," he said. "That I cannot re-
pay. I give you these small things to show you that I
value your friendship. I hope nothing ever comes between your people and mine."

"We go," Wolf Walker said.

"Go. One day I shall come to see you again. I shall
come to your lodge."

"You will be welcome. My fire is yours."

He watched them ride away, straight backs dark
against the sunset.

He swung his horse and rode back to town. Back to
the haunts of men, the bargaining places, and the risks
that attend living among rough and violent men. But he
was at home now. This was his country.

And now he must see Doris. He must tell her of his
plans.

The lights were on in the town. The great tents

glowed with the lights inside, and black shadows moved across their canvas walls. Music came from within, and the click of poker chips and a roulette wheel.

Men leaned against the lamp posts topped off with lanterns, or thronged the muddy streets, churned by hoofs and boots. Horsemen rode by; other horses stood three-legged and sleepy at the hitching rails. He led his horse to a place near where he had bunched his cattle, and picketed it on good grass.

A man came out of the darkness and stood near him. It was Mobile Callahan.

"I figured you were dead," Chantry said.

"No. I've been about my business."

"Which is?"

"Keepin' folks off your back."

Ignoring the remark, Chantry asked, "Where's Bone? Did he make it?"

"Yeah. The cattle carried us west. We figured we'd better sit tight, after roundin' up a few. There was trouble brewin' here, and we knew you'd want Earnshaw and his girl looked after."

"You were right. What danger are they in?"

"They're close to you? That makes it enough. There's some folks don't give up easy, and one of them is that she-cat Sarah."

"She's here?"

"She's here all right, and the Talrims are with her. And they ain't all. She's teamed up with two other galoots. Seems they are the ones who killed your pa."

"There were three."

"Two now. Only one of them's got some boys as mean as he is."

He listened to the music, heard a loud laugh and the jingle of spurs, hard heels on a boardwalk . . . the only stretch of walk in town, in front of the general store, the biggest hotel tent, and a gambling place.

"Where is Earnshaw?" he asked.

Callahan nodded toward the siding. "Private car, yonder. He came west with a friend of his, a railroad man."

Chantry turned to go. "Watch your step," Callahan warned. "They know you're in town. They know they've got to kill you."

"Where's French?"

"Nobody has seen him. The word is that he pulled his men away from you, figured you'd never get the herd in without him, and then he would have the herd if the Kiowas didn't get it. I heard that some of his boys didn't want to leave you, but he took them anyhow."

"I hope that's right. I liked those boys."

Chantry walked back to the street. He stood for a moment against the side of one of the frame buildings, looking up and down the street. It was crowded, any of those men might be the ones who sought him. He stepped out from the shadows and made his way between the scattered tents toward the siding where the private cars waited. Lights showed from their windows.

He studied the layout with care, but no one seemed to be about. Fifty yards or so away were a dozen empty boxcars and some flatcars, and beyond them the stockpens and a loading chute.

After a moment he crossed the open space to the nearest of the private cars and, grasping the handrail, swung up the steps to the platform at the rear. The door was of frosted glass, and he rapped gently.

The door opened and a white-coated Negro showed him into a comfortable lounge of plush-covered furniture, crystal chandeliers, Venetian mirrors, looped and fringed draperies, and antimacassars.

Doris Earnshaw was seated on a sofa, a book in her hand. At the sound of his voice she rose hurriedly and came to meet him.

For a moment she looked at him in astonishment. "Tom! How you've changed!"

He grinned. "I need a bath," he said. "I just got in off the range."

"But . . . but you've *changed!* You're bigger, older, browner . . . everything!"

"Part of it will wash off. Out where I've been, having a bath isn't a simple thing."

Earnshaw came in. "Tom! Am I glad to see you! How are the cattle!"

"We brought most of them in. Around two thousand head, give or take a few."

"What did you pay for them?"

He explained as briefly as possible. "Then the herd is ours?" Earnshaw said. "It all seems unbelievable."

"Out here," Chantry said, "almost everything is."

Earnshaw listened as he told of the beef situation and the conditions in the area. "I can get twenty-two dollars a head for your stock right now, if they are in good shape," he said. "What would you say to a quick sale right here, then buy another herd to ship east to our own plant?"

"Fine."

He was thinking of the street out there, and what remained for him to do. "I'd prefer that you two stay in the car," he said, when Earnshaw had finished outlining his plans. "Let me handle the outside business. This is a pretty rough place."

"I gathered as much," Earnshaw said dryly. He gave Chantry a quick, searching glance. "What is this I hear about you?"

"Things are very different out here, sir." He indicated the street. "Every man out there carries a gun. I expect you've heard some shooting." He hesitated. "There are several men out there, and at least one woman, who want to kill me."

He could see they did not believe him. "That's silly!" Doris said. "Why would—" She broke off. "Tom, you're serious. You mean it."

"Yes, I do."

"A Mr. Sparrow told me something of the sort," Earnshaw said, "but it all seemed rather melodramatic."

"Mr. Sparrow," Chantry replied, "is a businessman. He is a cattleman and a rancher, and from all I gather, a very successful one."

"He is certainly interested in you," Earnshaw commented. "He assured me you were quite a remarkable young man."

"But we knew that, didn't we, Papa?"

Earnshaw studied him. "You've changed, Chantry. I don't know what it is about you."

"I've survived, that's what it is. I think periods of change are rather drastic out here, as compared with what happens in the East."

When Earnshaw had retired to the sleeping compartments Doris came closer. "Tom, you mentioned a woman. What is she like?"

He shrugged. "I don't know," he said honestly. "I actually met her only once, and we weren't exactly introduced. I don't even know her last name; her first name is Sarah. She is here in town, I hear, and she seems to believe that my death would be advantageous. My advice to you is to keep your door locked at all times. Don't let anyone in unless you know them well."

He paused a moment. "Doris, your father mentioned a quick sale. Whom did he have in mind?"

"Colonel Enright. His car is right behind ours. He is here to buy beef, and he will pay cash . . . in gold."

Chantry sat on the edge of the plush sofa, his hat in his hand. He was restless and uneasy. Was it the sudden change of surroundings? Was it only that he needed a bath, a change of clothes? Or was it the knowledge that out there in the dark trouble awaited him, trouble he could not avoid.

Slowly, almost thinking out loud, he reviewed for Doris all that had happened. When he had finished, she said, "What will she do now? You have the cattle here. You are alive, and possibly Mr. Williams is alive too. So what can she do?"

"If you were she, what would you do?"

She answered quickly. "I'd go for the money. When you sell the cattle, I'd steal the money."

He considered that. Until now Sarah had been working to inherit the cattle and sell the herd herself, and she had balked at nothing . . . nothing at all.

Yes, he agreed reluctantly, she would steal the money. She would do just what Doris had suggested.

He knew what the trouble was, for he had a touch of it himself. There was a feeling here that this was somehow out of the world, that what one did in the West belonged only to the West, and when one left, it could be left behind. Of course, that was not true. But . . . hadn't it been true for some people?

So many of them had that idea. They came to get rich and get out.

Chapter 20

When he left the private car, Tom Chantry moved quickly to the shadow of a pile of lumber. There, crouching in the darkness, he waited and watched.

He had been in the West only a short time, but it was true that circumstances had changed him. He had grown more watchful, less trusting of people or appearances. He had enemies of whom he knew little except that they seemed prepared to stop at nothing. He had some friends, but he could not feel entirely sure who were friends and who were enemies. He would do well to play out his hand as if he were alone, and without help.

Undoubtedly Earnshaw wanted to make a quick deal, a quick profit that would put him on his feet once more. Then there could be the purchase and shipment of a second herd that would launch him into business again. That made sense, and this was the place to do it.

But Sarah was in town, and she had with her the Talrims, who killed without qualm or hesitation. Apparently she had also established a working arrangement with the killers of his father. These were his enemies, persons to whom his death seemed a necessity.

The area covered by the town, even with the scattered piles of building materials, corrals, and freight cars, was small, and his enemies would be moving in and around that area; there was small chance of avoiding them. He must locate their headquarters, for there had to be a focal point.

He thought of Mobile Callahan, who had helped him, paid to do so by Sparrow . . . why? For the time being he would dismiss that, while keeping it in the back of his mind. No matter what the motive, this did not present any immediate danger.

Bone McCarthy was, he believed, still working for

him. Of Sun Chief there had been no sign, and it seemed likely that he had been killed in the stampede. And where was French Williams? Knowing the man, Chantry was sure he would not give up without a fight.

Crouching and waiting to see if he had been followed, or if anyone was watching the car, he considered his situation.

Sparrow's warning had been a good one. He must avoid further shooting if possible. What he had to do was simple enough. He must bring the sale of the cattle to Colonel Enright to a conclusion, get the money into Earnshaw's hands, effect the purchase and shipment of a second bunch of cattle, and then get out.

Though a move now against the herd was possible, it was unlikely. Doris' conclusion, he felt sure, was the right one. Sarah would be apt to make an attempt to get the purchase price into her hands. So . . . the car must be guarded against any such attempt.

He must get Enright and Earnshaw together at once, and effect the sale and the transfer of money. And then he had to find a herd of cattle available for purchase within a reasonable distance of the railroad.

All this he had to do while avoiding trouble with any of his enemies. He was going to need eyes in the back of his head.

Sarah would wait until she found out the payment had been made for the cattle, and she would keep the Talrims in check until then . . . at least, that was the way he saw it. With him out of the way, the whole affair might be moved along quickly.

He straightened up and went around a tent and between two piles of lumber to the street. He stopped there, scanning the street carefully.

It was likely that this town was only temporary. This was for a brief time the end of the tracks, and when they built them on west, the town itself would move too. Everything here was set up to be torn down. The camp of the construction workers was a mile further west even now; but the whiskey, the women, and the gambling were still here.

The street was scarcely two hundred yards long, with

frequent gaps. There were occasional piles of lumber, stacks of goods covered with tarpaulins, wagons drawn up, back end to the street. At least fifty men were walking or standing along the street, most of them only dark figures, and any one of them might be an enemy. The tents and shacks were jammed to the doors with men.

Chantry waited a moment, then crossed the street and made his way back to the herd.

Bone McCarthy was squatting by the fire. "Gettin' worried about you, boss. I nigh come a-huntin' you."

"Who's out there?"

"Four cowhands from town. All of 'em busted and glad for the work. Good men, too. I punched cows with two of 'em down on the Brazos one time."

"Bone, I want you to guard that private car where Earnshaw and his daughter are." He explained the situation, and added, "There's just the two of them and a man named Whitman. He's out here for the railroad, and the private car is his. I don't expect any trouble until the gold is transferred from Enright to Earnshaw. I understand that Enright has a couple of tough railroad detectives guarding his car on the inside."

"Have you seen French?"

"No."

Bone filled his cup. "Worries me, that does. It ain't like him to give up."

With the cattle guarded and Bone McCarthy taking over the job of watching over Earnshaw and Doris, Chantry had made his first move in the events that were shaping up.

He left McCarthy and went to the general store, where he bought a new outfit, with several extra shirts and pairs of pants. He selected a new pistol, oiled it well, and tried the balance. He loaded his belt with cartridges, filling all the empty loops, and then, carrying his purchases, he went to the barber shop, where he got a shave and a haircut. He went back to the private car and asked for the use of the bath. He scrubbed and soaked, and came out wearing fresh clothes and feeling clean for the first time in days.

When he glanced outside the car window there was no one in sight. A minute later Colonel Enright appeared with Earnshaw.

"I've been looking at your cattle, young man. They're in good shape. I'd buy another herd of the same size at the same price."

"We'll see what we can do," Chantry said.

Then they discussed the price, and it was finally settled at twenty-two dollars per head—more than he had expected, much more than Sarah had hoped for. In round numbers it came to forty-five thousand dollars in gold.

"You'll have to come and get it," Enright said, and added, "Once that gold is out of my hands it is your responsibility—and if I were you I'd have myself ready for trouble."

"We'll be all right," Earnshaw said. "I don't expect any trouble."

Chantry walked out on the brass-railed observation platform. Bone McCarthy was loitering nearby and he strolled over.

"You stay where you are, Bone," Chantry said. "Keep an eye on things and don't let anybody get behind you."

"All right."

Chantry went back inside. "Doris, keep the door of the car locked while we're gone, but be prepared to open it quickly to get your father inside."

"Do you think they will try to steal the gold?"

"You figured it out last night—remember? I think you were right."

They talked quietly, and of many things, but always his ears were alert for other sounds. Earnshaw came from the inner room and stood waiting.

Chantry looked up. "Now?"

"Yes."

"It might be safer to wait until daylight."

"They wouldn't attempt a robbery right here in the middle of everything. I think we're safe enough, Tom. Let's go."

Reluctantly, Chantry got to his feet. He opened the door. "Excuse me," he said, and stepped out first.

All was quiet. On the street, perhaps sixty yards away, there were the usual sounds. Occasionally a wild cowboy yell would leap from the jumble of sound and hang in air for an instant.

A dozen yards away was a pile of lumber, and beyond it, much further off, were several boxcars and tents. Tom went down the steps facing forward, and stepped off. There was no sign of Bone McCarthy, but he had expected none. Earnshaw came down the steps after him and together they walked back beside the track to Enright's car.

Inside it was just as ornate as the other. Two tough-looking eastern men loafed in the drawing room with a pair of shotguns across the table before them. They had been playing checkers.

At a call from one of them, Enright came from the sleeping room, bringing a sack of gold. He returned for another, then made more trips until there were eight sacks in all.

"That's a fair load," he said. "You'll have to make more than one trip."

Chantry liked none of it. One trip, loaded down with gold, was bad enough, but several? With each step the odds piled up against them, and no matter what they carried each man must keep one hand free to use a gun.

He glanced at the two guards. "You two want to help? We'll pay you."

One man shook his head. "Mister, I've got a family back in St. Louis. I wouldn't stick my head out of that door with a sack of gold for anything on earth."

"Nor me," said the other. "Guarding inside of this car is one thing. The Colonel here, he's got steel plates in the sides of this car. He's ready for anything that happens. From in here we could stand off an army, but outside there in the dark? Mister, maybe I'm not very bright, but I'm not crazy, either."

"Besides," he added, "we've heard all the talk. I'd like to help you, but I just can't see my way clear to committing suicide."

Earnshaw stared at them, then he looked at Tom. For the first time he appeared to realize the gravity of the situation. "Is it that bad?" he asked.

"Mr. Earnshaw," Chantry said, "out there tonight in that cluster of shacks and tents are perhaps a hundred men who have committed every crime in the books. They come here to prey on the track-workers, but they'll grab anything that's loose. Aside from them, there are at least two groups who feel they should have this money. One of them has already killed men in the process of trying to steal the cattle. They are not in town just to have a little recreation."

"It's only a few yards," Earnshaw said. "We'll move it now."

Chantry bent over and looked out of the car windows. All was dark and silent. There was a faint glow of light from the windows of the car they were in, and he could see light from the other private car further along the track. There might be any number of men hidden out there, and they could remain invisible until they opened fire.

"We'll cover you from the door," one of the guards volunteered, "but that will help for only a few yards."

Chantry picked up two of the sacks and slung them over his left shoulder. In his right hand he carried his gun. Earnshaw took two sacks and they stepped out of the door.

Chantry went down the car's steps and dropped off to the dirt. This was, he felt, the crucial moment. Nothing happened.

He moved out, gun ready, and waited until Earnshaw reached the ground. With Earnshaw close behind him, he started for the other car.

Three hours earlier, and a few hundred yards from town on the bank of the Arkansas, three big men got down from their horses, tied them to brush, and descended a steep path to the door of a dugout in the river's bank.

The door of the dugout was above the water-level and some distance back from the river's edge, but the dugout had been the work of some optimist who was ignorant of western rivers. The Arkansas in flood was far from being the placid stream that now flowed along not far from the door. In flood it was another story; at the first high water the dugout would be flooded, washed out and away. At the moment, four people sat inside awaiting the arrival of the three big men.

A table, two benches, and four bunks were in the small room. Hank Talrim was sprawled on one of the bunks, chewing on a straw. Bud was at the end of the table, watching Sarah, who was playing solitaire.

The fourth person was a tall, slim man with an oddly twisted look to his face. He was sallow and unshaven, and his mustache was stained with tobacco. There was an expression about him of ingrown bitterness and distaste.

The door opened and all of them looked up. The man who entered first was huge, with broad shoulders and big hands; his once red hair was freely sprinkled with gray.

"Howdy." He glanced once at Sarah, then at the sallow-faced man. "Hello, Harvey. You seen Sparrow?"

"Sparrow? Is he here?"

"Uh-huh. What you reckon that means?"

Harvey shrugged. Ruff always irritated him. It was the man's size. They had worked together a dozen times over the years, but Harvey never failed to be angered by Ruff's very presence. And now to make things worse, there were the two boys as well, huge men too.

"Maybe he's here same as us. If Chantry's boys is huntin' us he surely ain't goin' to have to look far."

"Stay away from him!" Sarah said curtly. "He'll get his when we get the gold. Leave it at that, and stay out of sight."

"I still say the best time is when they are transferring the gold from one car to the other," Harvey said.

"And that's why you've got nothing," Sarah replied sharply. "They will be keyed up, ready for trouble. Chantry will have some men around, some we don't expect to be there. Let them move the gold. We'll take it when they're off guard and think they can relax."

"What d'you think?" Frank Ruff looked at Bud Talrim.

"I like her thinkin'. What she says, goes."

Ruff sat down, and the two boys, Mort and Charlie, squatted on their heels. "I don't like it, Sparrow bein' here. He's always been sore over that shootin'."

"Forget him!" Harvey said. "He never amounted to nothin'."

"Have you seen him lately?" Charlie Ruff spoke mildly. "He's mighty high-toned now, got him a big ranch down Texas way, and another in New Mexico. He runs fifteen, twenty thousand head of cattle."

"I don't believe it," Harvey said.

"Believe whatever you're of a mind to," Charlie said. "That's a fact, what I said."

"Some of those cattle Williams and Chantry were drivin' were his," Mort Ruff commented. "Sparrow's in this somehow."

"Maybe if we wait," Frank Ruff said, "he'll do our killin' for us."

For a few moments there was only the sound of the shuffling of the cards.

Then Sarah spoke. "Those cattle," she said, "will bring nearly fifty thousand dollars."

"I never seen that much money," Hank Talrim said. "Somehow it don't make no picture."

Bud gave him a disgusted glance. "You can make a picture out of a dollar, can't you? Well, anything you can buy with a dollar, you can buy fifty thousand times as much."

"Whoo-ee!" Hank exclaimed. "I don't know what I'd do with it all."

Sarah's face was still. Only her eyes seemed to move, and they missed nothing. Secretly she felt only contempt for these men, but they were useful to her. And she did not underrate them. The Talrims seemed willing to do what she said, but they would turn on her and kill her as quickly as a cat. The others, she was sure, would not kill a woman.

As she played she studied them, considering which one she would need the most. Once the money was in their possession, she must get rid of the Talrims. Harvey was as treacherous as the Talrims, and Frank Ruff was too suspicious. Charlie was the smartest of the lot, the best-natured, the only one around whom she felt safe, but at the same time she believed he would be less easy to fool.

Mort was the one. Somehow she would have to work on Mort . . . she had caught him stealing glances at her. And somehow she must trigger trouble between Harvey and the Talrims . . . after they had the gold.

Once Paul was gone, she had moved at once to use the Talrims. She had crossed their trail a few times, knew where they were likely to be, and she had approached them, demanding their help. She was still not sure why they had gone along, nor did she dare approach either one separately. Each one seemed aware of what the other was thinking, and she was intelligent enough to perceive that there was no separating them.

They had told her about Rugger. He was a cow thief, and worse. So she had waited for him one night on night guard around the herd. She kept out of sight until he appeared, led him off to one side, and suggested stealing the herd. The others had come in as a matter of course.

When the theft failed she saw at once that the death of French Williams was no longer important. They were too close to the railhead, and the thing to do was get the money after the herd had been sold. She intended to have that money and to go to England or France with it and live her years out in style.

She was sure that at least one and probably two of the men helping her would be killed. And a fight between Harvey and the Talrims would not be difficult to start . . . eliminating one or two.

She had no clear plan, but she had a driving desire and the ability to move quickly when the moment came. She was ready.

Chapter 21

Tom Chantry sat on the car steps, staring into the night. The gold—all of it—had been carried from one car to the other without trouble.

Earnshaw was pleased, and mildly triumphant. "See? I knew nothing would happen. We're perfectly safe."

Chantry glanced at him, then looked away. Doris had been silent, but presently she said, "Well, I was wrong, too. I was sure that girl would get them to try to steal the gold when it was being moved."

"Maybe they're not so bad as we think," Earnshaw said mildly. "Tom, I'm afraid you frightened us all needlessly."

"I don't think so," Chantry said stubbornly. "They've just made other plans."

After that he had gone outside and sat down. Doris was going to bed, Earnshaw was shaving. Suddenly Bone McCarthy came out of the darkness, and a moment later, Mobile Callahan.

"What happened?" Bone wondered.

"They're not around town," Callahan said. "I've been keeping my eyes and ears open. None of them's around, and none of them's been seen. By morning, if they're still here I'll know where they are. I've got the kids looking for them."

"Kids? Here?"

"Sure. There's a couple dozen of them in camp. I got some of them together and promised I'd buy them some rock candy if they locate that crowd, and if they're here those kids will find them."

They talked for a while, discussing possibilities. Neither McCarthy nor Callahan believed that Sarah and the Talrims would give up. Finally Tom went inside and went to sleep on the sofa in the car's drawing room, with the door locked and a chair under the knob, his pistol beside him.

For three days events moved without a hitch. Colonel Enright had the herd loaded and shipped. McCarthy and Chantry, riding wide over the country, located a small herd bound east for Dodge and arranged for purchase at the railhead. On the fourth day they found another herd after learning it was being held on a range north of the river for fattening.

Mobile remained in town. He gambled a little, talked a little, listened a lot. Twice he glimpsed Harvey on the street, and Sarah moved into the frame hotel and began making herself known around the area.

She was polite, reserved, well-behaved. To Mobile, who had learned much during his lifetime, it was obvious what she was doing. She was establishing a reputation for being a lady, a well-behaved lady interested in finding a brother who had disappeared somewhere in Colorado.

Under the circumstances she was free to talk to anyone, in search of information, and if she was seen in conversation with the Talrims she could simply explain that she had heard they had information about her brother.

Tom Chantry was puzzled. Over dinner in the private car with Earnshaw, Whitman, and Doris he confessed: "I'm worried. I know they haven't given up."

"Tom, you're obsessed with this woman, whatever her name is, and with those men. If they had intended to do anything they would have done it when we moved the gold. We were vulnerable then."

"Yes, I know. And the fact that we're in a settlement wouldn't stop the Talrims. I am sure they have some other plan."

"I've seen the young lady about town," Whitman said, "and certainly I'd never suspect her of wrongdoing. From what I hear, she is searching for news of her brother."

"Her brother was killed by the Kiowas. She knows that, and knows when it happened."

"Does that seem likely? What would she be doing

here, then? A young woman like her would have no reason to spend her time in a place like this."

"Unless she planned on picking up a good bit of gold."

Whitman shook his head doubtfully and changed the subject. Tom could see that even Doris was becoming somewhat impatient with him, and he said no more, but he did a lot of thinking.

When they bought the two herds, amounting to fifteen hundred head, the amount of gold they had aboard the train would be seriously depleted. Did Sarah know of their plans, he wondered.

Mobile Callahan strolled up to him as he stood on the street. "Mr. Chantry," he said, "the kids got 'em spotted."

"Where?"

"In a dugout down on the river. The whole crowd is there, and give 'em a few more days and they'll probably be mean enough to kill off each other."

"No sign of French?"

"Not a sign."

"I haven't seen Mr. Sparrow."

Mobile Callahan made no reply for a moment, and then he said, "He's around." He added, "I don't quite see what he's up to. My job was to keep trouble off your back . . . why? What's his interest in you?"

"I don't know." Suddenly Tom was not thinking of Sparrow. "Mobile, I'm going to see Sarah."

"You're *what?*" Mobile stared at him. And without waiting for a reply, he said, "Take a tip from me and stay away from her. That woman's trouble."

"Nevertheless—There she is now."

She was looking every inch the lady, her skirts gathered daintily in one hand as she crossed the street. Men stepped aside for her and tipped their hats.

"Tom"—it was the first time Mobile had ever used his first name—"these folks would hang you to the highest tree if you so much as said a word against her. And don't think she hasn't planned it that way."

They could hear her heels on the boardwalk, and then she stopped behind them. "Mr. Chantry? It *is* Mr. Chantry, isn't it?"

"It is."

"I understand you sold your cattle, you and Mr. Williams?"

"I sold them. French Williams no longer has any share in them, Miss—?"

"Millier. Are you going back east now?"

"No." Suddenly he realized there could be only one reason why she would want to stop and speak to him. She wanted information. Coolly, he gave it to her. "We're buying more cattle. Prices have gone down somewhat, so we're going to reinvest."

For just an instant he saw the stunned apprehension in her eyes, an expression quickly gone. "Do you think that is wise? You seem to have done very well with the first cattle you bought, but why buy cattle when the price is down?"

"That's the time to buy. Back east the market is good. The problem is getting cars right here. Buying cattle means holding them for some time. However, we are in a position to get the necessary cars."

He shifted ground quickly. "I understand you are looking for your lost brother. He was killed by the Kiowas, as you know."

Several people were within listening distance, and at least one man turned sharply around to hear better.

"I know nothing of the kind!" she replied, and walked away.

Mobile looked after her, and said softly, "What are you trying to do, Chantry? Start something?"

What *was* he trying to do? But he knew . . . he wanted to force them to move. He wanted it over with, ended once and for all. He was tired of watching, tired of waiting. Now they knew the gold they wanted would soon be gone, spent on cattle. If anything would bring matters to a head, this was it.

"I'd like to be listening in when she gets that word to them," he told Callahan grimly.

He walked back to the private car. Enright had pulled out on the morning train and the track was clear. Thoughtfully, he considered the possibilities.

The cattle were being brought down for delivery. Whitman, owner of the car and Earnshaw's very good friend on the railroad, had arranged for cars. Once delivery was made, gold would be paid to the cattlemen who brought in the herds, and Earnshaw and Doris would be free to return east . . . and so would he.

He glanced at his reflection in one of the panel mirrors in the car. He saw there a tall, bronzed young man with wide shoulders, narrow hips, and a quietly commanding way about him. Above all, there was no softness. The hard riding on the plains had taken off the extra flesh, hardened what remained, and toughened his nature. He was a different man now.

Why go back east? There was money to be made in the cattle business, there was land to be had, and several times lately he had heard men speaking of western Colorado. They had built a railroad out there, too, in that land of mountains and meadows, of running streams and forests.

Doris was standing behind him. "Tom, what are you thinking of?"

He turned around. "Doris, how would you like to live out here? Further west, in the mountains?"

"Is that what you want?"

"I don't know. I think it is. This country has changed me. Maybe it has only brought me back to myself, back to what I should be. Yes, I do know. I want to stay."

"All right," she said, "we'll stay." She hesitated a moment. "Can I bring my things out from the East?"

"Whatever you like."

Suddenly he heard steps on the platform behind him, and he turned swiftly, looking toward the frosted glass door. There was a light tap.

"Who is it?"

"Callahan. Can you open up?"

Gun in hand, he opened the door. Mobile was alone. "All right," he said, "you did it. All hell's breakin' loose. Harvey was on the street tonight with Mort Ruff. Sarah Millier has been talking about buying cattle, maybe starting a brand of her own. I don't know what that means, but you can be sure she's got some bee in her bonnet."

"Any sign of the Talrims?"

"No . . . but I'd swear I caught a glimpse of French Williams. It was near the store, and I walked down that way, but there was nobody around."

Whitman and Earnshaw had come from the dining room. Chantry turned to the railroad man. "Any chance of getting a locomotive? We may want to move this car, and fast."

"The cars are on the siding a mile east of town," Whitman said. "As I understand it, the cattle are to be there for loading by daylight." He paused. "I can have an engine ready to move your car at any hour you wish."

"At four o'clock in the morning then. Move this car to the loading area. Maybe we can put through the whole deal before they realize what is happening."

Earnshaw smiled. "Tom, you worry too much. There won't be any trouble. Porter and Wills will be there with their cattle, we'll load them, pay them, and start east. Doris tells me you two want to be married. Well you can come east and be married there, even if you want to return here. Just don't worry. I think you're being overconcerned."

"You may be right. Anyway, humor me enough to say nothing about the move."

Outside he talked briefly to McCarthy and Callahan, and then headed for the street.

Would he know his father's killers? It had been so long ago, and he had only a glimpse of them then. But the big man he would surely know, for there weren't many like him. He walked down to the store, looking carefully around.

This was where Mobile Callahan thought he had seen French. What would Williams' role be in this? Would he try to get the gold for himself? He was a strange sort of man who did many things on impulse. He was ruled by whim, by impulsive likes and dislikes that seemed to follow no rule.

The street was crowded as usual. Chantry went into one of the huge gambling tents for the first time. It was filled with pushing, bearded, sweating humanity. His eyes roamed the room . . . not a familiar face in sight.

Suddenly, across the room there was one. Familiar, yet unfamiliar. A huge, red-haired young man loomed head and shoulders above the crowd. It was not the man who had helped to kill his father; he was too young. From the description this had to be Charlie Ruff.

Their eyes met. For an instant the smile left Ruff's eyes and he stared, hard-eyed, at Tom Chantry. Then the smile appeared again, and the big man came shouldering through the crowd, ignoring those he brushed against. Angry looks changed quickly when they saw the size of the man who had shoved them out of the way.

He stopped, wide-legged, in front of Chantry. "Howdy! You'll be Chantry. I've heard a lot about you."

Several heads had turned, watching.

"You've come a long way for what you're going to get," Charlie said, grinning. "You better tuck your tail an' run while you got a chance."

"And what am I going to get, as you phrase it?"

A big young man, secure in his huge size and strength, Charlie Ruff had walked through life with little trouble. There was no fear in him, and there never had been. Men stepped aside for him, or backed away. He liked it that way, and he was used to it.

But he guarded his words now. "You're going to get what you've got comin'," he said, "and I'm goin' to give it to you."

"Then why not now?" Chantry asked.

Charlie's grin stiffened a little. He had never been challenged before, never called to back up a threat. The games had come to a halt, people were backing away. Tom Chantry unbuckled his belt and handed it to a croupier. "Why not now, Charlie?" he said again.

Charlie Ruff was in a quandary. When he had started for town the last thing his father said was for him to stay out of trouble. "Watch a little, play a little, see if any of that crowd are around town, *but stay out of trouble!*"

It was too late to think of that now. He had wanted

to throw a scare into this man. He had wanted to push a little just to see the man back off, as others had done.

"Sure," he said, "why not now?" And he swung.

Charlie Ruff had thrown his huge fist with intent to demolish. Not a man in the room, with the exception of the croupier, who had seen many men and had learned how to judge them, and a couple of old-timers, expected anything but a quick, brutal beating. But what happened then Charlie Ruff was unprepared for.

Tom Chantry slipped inside of the ponderous right and smashed a right to the ribs. It was a beautifully timed punch and it landed solidly. Instantly he rolled and hooked a left to the same spot, then came back just enough and brought up a short, wicked uppercut to the chin.

Charlie Ruff went down, his breath knocked from him, his nose streaming blood.

He hit the dirt floor of the tent with a thud that shocked him through and through. Never before had he been hurt, never had he been knocked down.

He stared, then with a grunt he came off the ground and ran into two hard fists. The first split the skin under his eye, the second pulped his lips. But he was big and tough, and he kept coming. He reached out his huge arms and Chantry stepped back to get distance, but the crowd shoved him back. The huge arms caught him and enveloped him in a bear hug.

Charlie Ruff was a powerful man, and now he was wild with anger. He wanted to kill this man, to break him in two. With all his power he began to squeeze.

For one brief, agonizing moment Chantry thought he was gone. He felt a hard fist crushed against his spine, felt himself bent backward. Charlie Ruff was at least fifty pounds heavier, and much stronger.

There was one thing to do and he did it. He kicked up both feet and fell backward.

The sudden yielding fooled Charlie Ruff and he fell forward, stumbling in trying to catch his balance, losing his grip on Chantry as he did so.

Chantry was up and around in an instant. Charlie got his balance and turned, and caught a sweeping right to the jaw that knocked him against a tent pole. The whole tent trembled, and then the big man turned and came in, trying for his hold again.

Chantry stabbed a left to the mouth, and as Ruff lunged he side-stepped away from him.

For a moment they faced each other. For the first time Charlie Ruff knew fear.

He blinked through the sweat and blood at Chantry, standing there ready, lean, hard, and dangerous, waiting for him. Charlie Ruff had strutted and pushed and shoved all his life, smaller men had stepped away from him, appalled not only by the sheer size of him, but by the knowledge that where he was his father and brother were not far behind. But now they were not here, and he was alone.

The crowd was packed tightly around him. There was no place to run. He had felt those iron-hard fists, and he did not want to feel them again. The only way out was to kill Chantry. He was bigger, he told himself, and Chantry had been lucky so far. Slowly he began to circle, and Chantry turned coolly to face him as he moved.

Suddenly he charged, head down, arms flailing. A sweeping right smashed Chantry on the shoulder, staggering him and numbing his arm. The big man lunged into him, grabbing and pounding. Charlie knew nothing of fighting, but he had size and power.

His fists thudded and banged. Chantry staggered, shuddering under the power of Charlie's blows, and Charlie tried to smother him with sheer weight and size. Chantry went down, narrowly avoided a ponderous kick, then lunged up and caught Charlie with an overhand right. He slipped inside of a swing and smashed with both hands at the big body.

Pulling Charlie Ruff back, Chantry leaned into him and battered his body with short, wicked blows to the wind. Suddenly stepping back, he whipped up an uppercut that caught the bigger man under the chin. His head flew back and his knees buckled. Charlie hit the floor on his knees, but in the instant before he hit, Chantry swung a hard right to the jaw. Charlie fell forward on his face.

For a moment, Chantry stood looking down, and then he stepped back. The croupier held out his guns. "You'll be needing those." And he added, "I know that outfit. Watch yourself."

"Thanks."

Bloody, his shirt torn, Tom Chantry pushed toward the exit. He had wanted none of this. He had not liked Charlie Ruff, but he had not wanted to fight him; now it was done, and he had won.

Outside the cool wind chilled his sweaty body. He started up the street, wanting to get under cover, to bathe, and get into a clean, fresh shirt.

Chapter 22

He went to the frame hotel. The lobby was empty except for the clerk, an older man with a round, moon-like face.

"Hello, Mr. Chantry. Looks as if you've had trouble. Want a place to wash up?"

"Yes . . . and a shirt if you can rustle one up."

"I'll try. Come along." He led the way down a passage and into the back room on the ground floor. "There's a well out back. I'll get you a bucket of water. You'll want some hot water for those hands."

When he returned with the bucket and began kindling a fire in the stove, he asked, "What happened?"

"I had a fight. With Charlie Ruff."

The clerk whistled. "Ruff? You must have whipped him. You're not badly beat up."

"I did what I had to do."

"A lot of people will be pleased—not only here, but down in Texas too."

The clerk sat down. "My name's Finlayson. We haven't met but I've seen you around, and you're a friend of Mr. Sparrow's. Is there anything else I can do for you?"

Chantry was about to say there was not, but changed it. "One thing. What do you know about Sarah Millier?"

"Enough not to be so gullible as most of the local citizens. She had visitors, Mr. Chantry. Mostly they used the back stairs, but I saw them once or twice—the Talrims or Frank Ruff. She saw me noticing them once, and commented that they had some information on her brother."

Chantry explained about the brother, and gave some background on Sarah and Paul. "There's some connection with French Williams, but I don't believe it's friendly."

"I always liked French," Finlayson commented. "Well, I don't know what to think about her, but I'm glad she's gone."

"Gone?" Chantry straightened up, water dripping from his hair and hands.

"Checked out about an hour after sundown. There was a rig waiting out front. I didn't see who was driving."

Tom dried his face and hands, working gently over his bruised and battered knuckles. He worked his fingers to keep stiffness from settling in the muscles.

He was terribly tired, but there was no time to rest. After thanking the clerk, who refused payment, he went out and made his way to the corral. His horse was there, and he roped it and saddled up.

He swung into the saddle and turned his horse toward the siding where the private car was waiting. ... Only it was gone.

He rode to the main track, and looked around, but there was no car ... it had pulled out.

He swung his mount and raced across town, weaving in and out among the buildings, the tents and stacks of lumber, to the other sidings. A small shack was over there where relief engineers and other trainmen bunked.

Dropping from his saddle, he went in the door. A man turned sleepily in a bunk. "Who's that?" he muttered.

Chantry struck a match and lighted the lamp. "Whitman's private care is gone. Where is it?"

The man swung his feet to the floor. He was wearing red woollen long-johns, now faded to a vague pink. "Whitman's car? I'm supposed to take that out m'self. It's gone, you say? That can't be."

"Where's your engine?"

"On the siding. Right back yonder."

Both men rushed to the door. There was no engine. The siding was empty.

"Stole! Somebody stole the engine!"

He turned back into the room and yelled at the other

trainmen, now half awake. "The engine's gone! Somebody stole it!"

"It's Harvey!" A tall, skinny man started up. "I seen that outlaw Harvey aroun'! He used to be a trainman back Missouri way!"

Tom Chantry went to his horse. They had Doris! They had Whitman and Earnshaw too, and the gold, and they had a start of an hour or longer; but one thing about a locomotive . . . it had to keep to the tracks. Somewhere, not very far off, they would have horses waiting.

He started along the tracks at a canter. Where were McCarthy and Callahan?

A mile out of town the loading pens showed their skeleton frames against the sky, but there was no train. He pushed on, riding beside the tracks, watching the skyline ahead.

He had no idea what lay before him. That they would be stopping soon, he was sure. The outlaws would not dare risk going into the next station. He rode on into the night, his eyes probing at the darkness ahead.

Suddenly the shapes loomed up. The locomotive stood silent, except for a faint hiss of steam. The private car was lighted, but no sound came from it.

Slowing his pace, gun in hand, he circled the car at a distance. The hoofs of his horse made little noise as they moved through the grass.

He rode closer, then dismounted and ground-hitched his horse. Close to the car, he stopped to listen. No sound. He stepped up on the road bed, caught the rail, and swung up to the platform.

His left hand closed on the knob, turned it. The door opened easily and swung inward. The drawing room was empty, the door to the bedroom stood open. He went past it . . . empty.

There were signs here of hasty dressing; clothing was thrown about. The safe stood open, papers were scattered on the floor. They had the money, and they had Whitman, Earnshaw, and Doris.

He found a red lantern, lighted it, and hung it out on the east end of the locomotive. There were no trains west of this; the next to come would be from the east.

He searched the car, found two boxes of .44 cartridges, which he took, as well as an extra pistol, hidden under the pillow of Whitman's bed. He thrust that into his waistband. He gathered some food, found a canteen and filled it. He found a good deal of hunting gear in a closet under Whitman's bed, but nothing he could use. Outside, he stuffed the food into the saddlebags, hung the canteen around the pommel, and then scouted for tracks, using a lantern.

He found a place where horses had stood, several of them. And there was a faint trail leading off to the south.

For a moment, after he was in the saddle, he sat thinking. They must have taken the three prisoners so there would be nobody to tell who had taken the gold, or where they had gone. It was unlikely they would keep them for long. Sarah would be for killing them. She had intended to kill him back there under the trees in the rain, even though her brother had not wanted it. She would want no witnesses, and the Talrims would agree.

The Ruffs? No telling about them, they might agree, and they might just ride off and leave it to Sarah and the Talrims.

Just then he heard the pound of hoofs, and, turning, saw a rider approaching along his own trail. The man pulled up when he saw him.

"Chantry?" It was Sparrow.

"Here." Chantry held his gun, waiting. There were a lot of things about Sparrow that were unexplained.

"Are they gone?"

"Yes . . . and the money too."

"They'll ride south," Sparrow said. "I'm sure of it. They'll head for Coe's old hide-out."

"Do you know where it is?"

"No . . . only approximately. Nobody but outlaws knew where it was, but we can look."

"Maybe," said another voice, "you'd let me help."

They turned sharply, and faced a horseman who had come up quietly through the drift sand on the side of the track. It was French Williams.

"Howdy, Tom," he said, and Tom could almost see the taunting, appraising look in his eyes. "I see you got the herd through."

"No thanks to you," Chantry replied shortly.

"I wasn't supposed to help . . . remember? I will say that some of the boys set up a fuss when I pulled them off the herd. You make friends, d'you know that? Helvie, Gentry, and them, they swear by you."

"We've got a job to do," Chantry said. "Come along if you like."

"I'd better. No use lettin' you boys handle all that money. Nor the trouble, either." Williams turned his horse to ride along. "Surprised to see you here, Sparrow. I'd heard you were a man who avoided trouble."

"That has been my policy."

"Uh-huh. I recall. A changed policy now, is that it?" Williams chuckled. "You're the unlucky one, Chantry. You're ridin' alone, so to speak. Sparrow and me, we know where you stand, but you got no idea where we're placed in this setup. We can count on you; you don't know whether you can count on us or not."

"I'll fight my own battles. You stay out of it."

"Fire-eater, aren't you?" Williams said. "You sound a whole lot different from the fellow who backed off from Dutch Akin a while back. You got any idea what you're ridin' into?"

Williams, whether for his benefit or Sparrow's, had dropped into the casual, easy talk of many western men. He could speak well enough when he wanted to.

"I know. The Talrims, Harvey, and the Ruffs, six men, and a woman who's worse than all of them."

"You got any idea what kind of men they are? The Talrims, you know them. A couple of dirty-mean rattlesnakes. But Frank Ruff? Now there's something else. Frank Ruff could file twenty-seven notches on his guns if he was tinhorn enough to do it.

"You hear of men who've killed a few, but when you get to pinnin' it down to names and places you lose most of them. Not so with Frank Ruff. Him you can list for twenty-seven and you can find the names, dates, and places to match them, and ever' one of them standin' up and facin' him, one way or another. Mort, he's tallied about six, near as a body can figure, and Charlie about four, maybe five."

"Five," Sparrow said.

"So look at it any way you like, you're takin' on something more than a handful of pilgrims."

"You don't have to come."

"Wouldn't miss it. I got to see the boy who wouldn't draw against a drunken man face up to a pat hand like that, with Sarah for a joker in the deck."

They rode on then in silence. The sand dunes loomed, and Chantry swung his horse, riding up into them. Around a dune, and then he saw the buildings . . . two of them. Some scattered, weathered boards, a fallen-in roof . . . many tracks, but none that could be defined, because of the loose sand.

Chantry swung down and looked into the buildings. Nothing. Why had they stopped here, then?

"Chantry?" It was Williams. "Look here."

He emerged from the building and went toward Williams, who was around the corner, standing on the edge of a small pit.

In the bottom lay two bodies. Jumping down, he bent over, and saw that both the men there were bound and gagged, but very much alive. He untied the gags.

"They've got Doris," Earnshaw said. "If anybody follows they'll kill her."

"They will anyway," Williams said shortly. "Or leave her to the Talrims, which would be worse."

Hastily, they cut the men loose. Earnshaw stood up. "Go get them, Tom. For God's sake, find them in time! They left us here, said the sand would bury us in a few hours. Talrim said there was a storm coming up."

"The stars are going. Maybe he was right," Sparrow said. "Head back for the train. It's only a little way."

South again.

The air grew cooler. Clouds covered the sky.

"How far to Robber's Roost?" Chantry asked.

"Too far. They'll see this coming and head for shelter. It's going to be a gully-washer."

Tom Chantry was silent. In the last few moments an eerie feeling had been creeping over him. He knew where they were going, knew exactly.

"Do you believe in fate?" he asked Williams.

"I believe in a gun and a horse," French said, "and not much more."

Sparrow edged his horse over. "Why? What about it?"

"Two of the men who killed my father are in that bunch," he said. "And do you know where they're going for shelter? They're going to my old home—to Borden Chantry's ranch!"

Sparrow pulled up and came back. His voice was odd. "You mean the place up ahead belonged to your father? It was his land?"

"Yes, and he built the house."

They started on. He was coming right back to where he had barely escaped from the outlaws. Only now he was not driving cattle, or riding with anything on his mind but the men ahead . . . and Doris.

"How far behind them are we?" Sparrow wondered.

"We've gained—they stopped to leave Earnshaw and Whitman. They probably lost thirty minutes. And I don't think they are expecting pursuit . . . not yet, I mean."

A few spattering drops of rain fell. They drew up, got into their slickers, and rode on again. Occasionally there was a flash of lightning.

"They're walking their horses," French said. "We'll be gaining on them."

An hour passed . . . suddenly a light gleamed ahead, then vanished. Chantry thought of the house—the logs that had been pulled from the walls, the roof partly fallen-in. They would be in the house, and might not even know about the root cellar.

He led the way to the cottonwoods. Huge branches ran out from each tree and merged with others from nearby trees. Under them there was fair shelter from the rain, and when he was under them he stepped down from the saddle. The horses of the outlaws were outside the house.

"We'll have to wait until morning," Sparrow said.

"With the girl in there?" French said. "You're forgetting her, Sparrow."

"All right," Sparrow agreed. "When you're ready."

"We'll have to get them outside," Chantry said. "In close quarters she might be killed."

"They've started a fire," Sparrow commented. "I don't think they've been here long."

"Speaking of morning," Chantry said, "it's almost that now."

"You won't have to worry about your girl yet," French said cynically. "They'll split the money first."

"Look out! Somebody's coming!" Chantry warned.

They waited, their bodies merged with the trunks of the trees. Light showed as the door opened, and a girl stepped out. That would be Sarah.

She moved toward them, and stopped. A light showed again and a man appeared, a big man. He walked toward Sarah, stopping not much more than twenty feet away from them. "You wanted to see me?" He sounded puzzled. "It's Charlie the girls always want to talk to."

"I wanted to talk to you, Mort." Sarah's tone was soft, friendly. "I'm afraid, Mort. I'm afraid of the Talrims."

"Of them? They won't hurt you none. Besides, they got that other girl."

"I don't mean that. I'm afraid for all of us. You don't know them as I do. I'm sure they don't intend to divide that money with any of us. I was sure you would understand, Mort. Charlie is too . . . well, he doesn't seem as serious as you do."

"He laughs a lot, but Charlie's all right." Mort was obviously turning the idea over in his mind. "I don't take to them Talrims myself. I thought they were friends of yours."

"Oh, no. They sort of . . . well, they just joined up with me, and what's a girl to do? I couldn't drive them off, and I hadn't anybody to help me."

"I'll help you," Mort said earnestly.

"Be careful, then. Watch them. If they start for their guns . . ."

"Don't you worry none. I'm faster'n them. I'm faster'n anybody, except maybe pa."

"You go back in. If they say anything, you tell them

you like me—that you thought you might talk to me a little."

"All right. Only don't you worry none."

When he had gone, Sarah stood alone for a moment, and then, just as she turned to go back, French stepped out and said, "Sarah, it won't work."

She was calm. "Why not?"

"You'll be in there with them, Sarah, and if shooting starts, you're as likely to be shot as anyone."

French Williams started toward her, talking quietly. "Looking at the size of the place. There will be five guns going in there."

"Six," she said. "I'll do some shooting myself."

"Do you know who I am?"

"Of course. You've lost most of your accent, but it's there . . . I haven't seen you since I was a little girl."

He was close to her now. "You favor your father."

"You never liked him, did you? I can remember that."

"We didn't share the same ideas."

"I wonder if *we* do?"

"About that gold in there? I think so. You'd like to have it all, and so would I. You spoke of shooting. Who were you going to shoot?"

"Frank Ruff—who else? But not at first, not until he'd helped kill the Talrims." Her voice was matter-of-fact. "Mort will start it, and Charlie and their pa will have to back him. If anybody is left, I'll do the shooting."

She paused. "Or you can. After all, Uncle Henri, blood is thicker than water."

"Whose blood, Sarah? Surely not yours."

"Don't do it for blood them. Do it for the money. It is better that we have it than that they should."

"I'll agree to that," he said cheerfully. "But I will have no part of any shooting with that girl in there. She is the daughter of a .friend. Get her out first, then we will see."

She hesitated, and French Williams glanced toward the house. Soon they would be wondering what had become of her, and if they came out now . . .

"Wait. I'll see what I can do," and she turned and went back inside.

"Do you trust her?" Sparrow asked.

"Only to do what she thinks is best for her."

The sky was gray in the east. The rain, which had ceased, stood in pools like sheets of steel, and the leaves dripped. The clouds were breaking.

"They'll be moving soon," Sparrow warned. "They know that by this time the car has been missed, and the search will begin."

Sarah emerged from the house again, Doris beside her. Right behind them was Hank Talrim. As they walked toward the trees, Talrim watched them, then he went back inside.

Sarah stopped suddenly and Doris continued to walk ahead, moving toward a point just to the right of the trees and out of the line of fire.

Harvey stepped out the door, followed by Hank Talrim. "Hey!" Harvey yelled. "Come back here!"

As he shouted, Doris threw herself to the ground and rolled over into the shallow cut that led toward the spring.

Harvey started to run toward them when Talrim called out, "Harv! Wait!"

As Harvey turned, Hank Talrim shot him. He fell, and rolled over, and men burst from the house, guns in hand.

Hank laughed, and tilted his gun. He was ready to fire when Frank Ruff's big voice cut across the morning air with a shout. "No!" He pointed. "Look!"

All of them turned.

The morning sun had come from behind a cloud, and its light was reflected from a pool of rain water near the trees. It was enough to draw the eye.

French Williams stood there, and Tom Chantry and Sparrow.

For an instant no one spoke. Then it was Chantry, hoping, but not believing, that a shoot-out might be avoided. "Leave the money," he said clearly, "mount your horses, and ride out. We'll call it quits."

Frank Ruff ignored him. "Aren't you on the wrong

side, Sparrow?" he said. "Seems to me you should be over here with us."

"I am where I always should have been, Frank. You lied to me, you know."

Chantry was cool. He had an empty feeling inside, but his mind was clear, his eyes appraising. These were men of violence, and they would shoot. Even if Frank Ruff, older and perhaps wiser, might see the sense in just riding off, the Talrims would not.

Hank and Bud were the ones nearest the house. The three Ruffs were at the other side, scattered out, watching.

On his own side, Williams was a known gunfighter, a man of tested ability. He himself . . . well, he could shoot. As for Sparrow, he knew nothing about him except that the man was calm, controlled, and ready.

"You'd better do like the man says," Williams said, almost pleasantly. "You boys were never going to make it anyway. I've got four men between you and the hideout. They're coming up the country right now, scouting for sign."

They had forgotten Sarah.

Standing alone, she watched, her face cold and still, here eyes measuring. All she had come west for, all she had bargained for, all she wanted was in that house. The first part of her plan had begun to work when Hank Talrim had shot Harvey . . . that was one less. She had talked to the Talrims in confidence, and she had talked to Mort. No matter how it turned out, there would be fewer among whom to divide the loot.

According to her thinking, when the Ruffs burst into the open and saw Harvey down, they should have turned their guns on Hank; and in turn Bud would have started shooting. With her own gun to account for Frank Ruff, if need be—or whoever survived. . . .

It could still work. Williams and Chantry and Sparrow . . . the Talrims and the Ruffs . . . when it was all over she might still be alone.

She stood for an instant, knowing that the slightest move might start the shooting. She was hesitating, trying to decide what could be done that would be best for her, when Chantry spoke again.

"There need be no shooting here," he said quietly. "As you gentlemen know, I am against violence. Leave the gold, Ruff—just take your horses and ride out of here."

"What about your pa?"

"My father faced his problems in his time. I shall face mine in my time. What you did to my father was murder, Ruff. I have a feeling you will hang—if not for that, for some other crime. I see no reason for me to kill you, when your end is inevitable."

"You talk mighty fancy," Frank Ruff said. "All I hear is that you want to back out."

"I did not come hunting you. That was your own idea. I came west to buy cattle, as these men can testify. I have bought my cattle.

"You now have two sons. No matter who wins, the odds are that when the shooting is over you will have one less, maybe two less. Is that what you want?"

"He's right, Frank. It's a Mexican stand-off," Sparrow said.

Sarah saw only one thing. Frank Ruff was hesitating. The last argument had reached him. In a moment he might decide to quit, then there would be no shooting, and the gold would go to Chantry.

She knew the Talrims. Their first instinct, always, was to kill. If she moved at this tense moment, her move would draw the eyes of the others, and she knew what the Talrims would do then.

"Hank?" she said softly, and moved suddenly.

Eyes swung toward her, and the Talrims grabbed for their guns.

All eyes had turned but Tom Chantry's. Even as the Talrims drew, his gun was coming up. His first shot caught Hank Talrim in the stomach and knocked him to the ground; the second hit Bud in the shoulder.

And then a thunder of guns, stabbing flame. A man running, a man falling . . . a grunt, a scream, and then silence.

How long had it been? Only a few seconds. Tom Chantry still held his gun up, ready. But it was all over. So many lives, so short a time.

He could hardly realize yet what had happened.

From the corner of his eye he had seen French Williams . . . his gun had come out so fast it seemed almost to materialize out of thin air into his hand, spouting flame. Now Williams was down, hunched against a tree, his eyes still bright, his gun still ready, but his shirt was slowly turning crimson.

Sparrow was leaning against another tree, a trickle of blood on his cheek, more blood on his shirt.

Hank Talrim was dead. Bud was crawling toward his horse, but anybody could see he wasn't going far. Frank Ruff was dead, literally shot to pieces by French Williams. Mort Ruff was seemingly unhurt, and was bending over Charlie, who was down.

Doris came from the ditch where she had been lying. "Tom, are you all right?" she asked.

"I think so. Take care of French."

He went over to Sparrow. "Better get your coat off, Mr. Sparrow. I'll want to look at your side."

"It's just a crease. Tom, did you hear what Frank said? About me being on the wrong side?"

"So? I think you were on the right side."

"You don't understand, Tom. I want you to understand. I was a youngster . . . only sixteen. I'd been working with Frank Ruff and Harvey. They told me there was a man needed killing, that he'd killed a friend of theirs, and they wanted me to join them. I believed them, and I went along, and I didn't know what I was shaped up for until it happened. I didn't figure on an ambush, Tom. I didn't even know your father, but I helped shoot him down, and it wasn't until I read it in the papers and heard folks talking that I realized what I'd done.

"They lied to me, Tom, but I went along—maybe because I wanted them to think me a big man. I wanted to show them I had as much nerve as anyone. I didn't know until afterwards that the man I had helped to kill was a good man, a better man than any one of us."

"We'll consider your part past and done with now." And Chantry uncovered Sparrow's wound.

It was a crease, but a deep one. He tore the shirt

and made a pad, then bound it over the wound. There was nothing much else to be done here.

"I tried to make it up to you, Tom. I tried to help."

"You did."

Then Mobile Callahan and Bone McCarthy came riding hard down the slope. And from the south, came Hay Gent, McKay, and Helvie.

Chantry went over to French. "How is he?" he asked Doris.

"He's been shot three times—low on the left side, through the thigh, and the chest muscle on the left side where it joins the shoulder."

"They were shooting for his heart."

French looked up at him. "I've got no heart, Tom. That's why they couldn't hit it."

Callahan dropped from his horse and brought his saddlebags with him. "Let me at him. I've had something to do with this sort of thing."

McCarthy and Helvie were looking at the outlaws. Mort Ruff got slowly to his feet. "Charlie's hurt bad," he said. "Can you help him?"

"I'll try," Helvie said.

Bud Talrim was dead.

"We'd better report this," Chantry said.

Sparrow looked at him. "To whom? There isn't any law within a hundred and fifty miles that I know of. You report it if you like. I'm going to forget it."

McKay and Gent were pulling poles from the roof of the house. "We'll make some travois, like the Indians use," McKay said. "Carry the wounded back."

"I can ride," Sparrow said. "We'll need just two, for Williams and Charlie Ruff."

Suddenly Doris looked up. "Where's Sarah?"

Chantry looked blank. Nobody had thought of Sarah. She was gone. Two horses were gone, and the money was gone.

Mobile started for his horse. "We'll find her. Come on, Bone."

"All right if I come?" Helvie asked.

They rode out, and Chantry watched them go. Somehow the money did not seem so important now, although he knew it was. It was Earnshaw's future, Doris' future, and his.

But was it? They could start over. Out here that was possible. A setback was only that. Nothing to put a man down. You took such things, accepted them, and went on from there. It was a matter of the mind, that was all. If you weren't whipped in your mind, nothing could whip you.

"Let's get on with it," Tom Chantry said. "Back to the railroad."

Had there ever been a time when he was not riding toward the railroad?

Chapter 23

Sarah Millier was vastly content. She was safely away with two horses and all the gold. She had a good rifle, a pistol, and a map.

The map showed the location of the Arkansas River, it showed Trinidad to the west, Tascosa to the southeast. It was drawn on a piece of tablet paper, and Tascosa looked reassuringly close.

There was a stage from there to Fort Griffin and points east, and her horses were fresh. She would ride to Tascosa, catch the stage, go east to the railroad, then to New York; and within a matter of a few weeks she would be in Paris with nearly fifty thousand dollars in gold.

Nothing on the map said anything about the Llano Estacado . . . the Staked Plain.

Nor did it mention distance, nor the factor of time. She had just asked a man in Trinidad to show her how the places lay in respect to each other. She had said nothing to him about the fact that she might want to ride over that country.

She had the gold and she was safely away, and if anyone had survived that shooting back there they would be having trouble enough without following her. She rode blithely south, and a little east.

The day was warm and pleasant, and she made good time. By nightfall, when she camped on Wild Horse Creek, she had put twenty-five miles behind her.

There was a good bit of water in Wild Horse Creek, and she drank and her horses drank. There was food in the saddlebags, so she ate. Another hard day's ride, she thought, and she would be in Tascosa. That was the way it looked on her map.

Sarah had no canteen, nor did she realize the need for one. She had no idea that Wild Horse Creek was more often dry than otherwise. The next day she started out at daybreak, alternately walking or cantering.

At noon she was far out on a wide plain of sparse grass, with nothing in sight anywhere. Her horse no longer cantered, but was content to walk. A light wind began to blow, the sky was clear, the sun warm. She was thirsty, but unworried. When she saw brush ahead she knew it was a creek. Half an hour later she sat her horse in the dry bed of that creek. There was no water, no sign of any. She pushed on.

The pack horse carrying the gold lagged, and impatiently she tugged on the lead rope.

She rode on, into the sun-lit afternoon. Tascosa could not be far away now. The distance on the map the man had drawn had seemed so small, and she had no idea that she would never see Tascosa, that it was far away beyond the horizon, beyond many horizons, and that in all the land between water was scarce, even for those who knew where to look. Shortly before sundown she came upon the bones of cattle, and after that she saw them frequently.

Finally, unable to go on, she got down, tied her horse to several skulls pulled together, and slept. Before morning she awoke. Her throat was dry, and she was scarcely able to swallow.

She walked until the sun came up, then got into the saddle. She could see that her horses were suffering, the pack horse most, for the gold was heavy and a dead weight.

When the sun was high she looked all around her, and saw nothing but an endless plain, level as a floor, it seemed. She found water holes where the earth was cracked from the heat, but no water.

She came at last to a river bed. Instantly, her heart leaped with excitement. Tascosa was on the Canadian. This must be it! She was going to make it, after all!

The bed was dry.

The Cimarron, still far to the north of the Canadian, was often dry. She turned upstream, and after plodding for some distance she found a small pool behind a natural dam formed of rocks and brush. She drank. The water was bad, but she drank. And the horses drank, and the water was gone. In the shade of some brush she lay down to rest, after tying the horses to the brush.

She slept like something dead, then was awakened by the sun on her face.

The pack horse was gone. The branch to which it had been tied was broken. Her horse, tied more securely, had not gotten free.

There was a myriad of tracks of buffalo or cattle or something. Among them all she could not make out which were those of the horse, for the sand was soft and left no well-defined print.

She rode on upstream, found another miniature pool, drank and let the horse drink, them scrambled him up the bank. Seeing a low knoll, she rode to the top.

She stared, and a dreadful emptiness crept into her, for wherever she looked there was nothing, only the vast plain that swept away to the horizon. Never in all her life had she seen or imagined anything like this. It was a vast brown sea, rolling endlessly away.

There was no movement anywhere, no sign of life.

Something seemed to shrink inside her. She no longer even thought of the gold, only of life. Nothing in all her years had prepared her for this.

Yet she must keep on. It could not be far. Surely, surely, it must be close.

She turned the horse down the slope and headed south.

On the fifth day, Mobile Callahan sighted the pack horse. It was standing alone, head hanging. When they rode up they could see the pack had slipped around until it was under the horse's belly.

They cut the pack away, gave the horse a drink from water poured into the crown of a hat, then dividing the gold between their horses, and leading the pack horse, they turned back.

Bone McCarthy, standing in his stirrups, looked all around. "Beats all," he muttered. "Where do you figure she thought she was goin'? Ain't nothing off that way for miles!"

"Lost, maybe. Only she surely held to her course."

"What d'you think?"

"Figure it out for yourself. She had no water with her, and besides, water's too far apart in this country. I'd say she was dead."

"Come on. Packin' all this gold we'll be lucky to make it back ourselves."

Thirteen years later, two cowboys hunting strays in the lonely lands where the Panhandle of Oklahoma gives way to the Panhandle of Texas, came on some bones.

"Hey, Sam. Looka here!"

Sam rode over, looked into the shallow place behind the clump of bear grass. "What d'ya know? Woman, too."

"White woman." The first cowhand indicated the twisted leather of a boot sole and heel. He held up a finger bone. On it was a gold ring with a diamond—or what looked like one.

"What would a white woman be doin' away off here?"

He looked around. Some of the bones had been pulled away by coyotes. There was no sign of a grave. Somehow she had come to this point, died here, and remained lying there until now.

"Ought to bury her," Sam said.

"With what? We got no shovel. Come on. We got miles to go an' we'll be late for chuck. If we're late the cook will throw it out."

"What about the ring?"

"Leave it with her. Maybe she set store by it. And anyway, she's got nothing else."

They rode away. The sound of their hoof-beats died away. The wind stirred, and a little dust drifted over the whitened bones, and then lay still.

ABOUT THE AUTHOR

LOUIS L'AMOUR, born Louis Dearborn L'Amour, is of French-Irish descent. Although Mr. L'Amour claims his writing began as a "spur-of-the-moment thing," prompted by friends who relished his verbal tales of the West, he comes by his talent honestly. A frontiersman by heritage (his grandfather was scalped by the Sioux), and a universal man by experience, Louis L'Amour lives the life of his fictional heroes. Since leaving his native Jamestown, North Dakota, at the age of fifteen, he's been a longshoreman, lumberjack, elephant handler, hay shocker, flume builder, fruit picker, and an officer on tank destroyers during World War II. And he's written four hundred short stories and over fifty books (including a volume of poetry).

Mr. L'Amour has lectured widely, traveled the West thoroughly, studied archaeology, compiled biographies of over one thousand Western gunfighters, and read prodigiously (his library holds more than two thousand volumes). And he's watched thirty-one of his westerns as movies. He's circled the world on a freighter, mined in the West, sailed a dhow on the Red Sea, been shipwrecked in the West Indies, stranded in the Mojave Desert. He's won fifty-one of fifty-nine fights as a professional boxer and pinch-hit for Dorothy Kilgallen when she was on vacation from her column. Since 1816, thirty-three members of his family have been writers. And, he says, "I could sit in the middle of Sunset Boulevard and write with my typewriter on my knees; temperamental I am not."

Mr. L'Amour is re-creating an 1865 Western town, christened Shalako, where the borders of Utah, Arizona, New Mexico, and Colorado meet. Historically authentic from whistle to well, it will be a live, operating town, as well as a movie location and tourist attraction.

Mr. L'Amour now lives in Los Angeles with his wife Kathy, who helps with the enormous amount of research he does for his books. Soon, Mr. L'Amour hopes, the children (Beau and Angelique) will be helping too.

A Special Preview of
the exciting opening pages of

BENDIGO SHAFTER

The new novel of the west by
LOUIS L'AMOUR

1

Where the wagons stopped we built our homes, making the cabins tight against the winter's coming. Here in this place we would build our town, here we would create something new.

We would space our buildings, lay out our streets and dig wells to provide water for our people. The idea of it filled me with a heartwarming excitement such as I had not known before.

Was it this feeling of creating something new that held my brother Cain to his forge throughout the long hours? He knew the steel he turned in his hands, knew the weight of the hammer and where to strike, knew by the glow of the iron what its temperature would be; even the leap of the sparks had a message for his experience.

He knew when to heat and when to strike and when to dip the iron into water; yet when is the point at which a group of strangers becomes a community? What it is that forges the will of a people?

This I did not know, nor had I books to advise me, nor any experience to judge a matter of this kind. We who now were alien, strangers drawn together by wagons moving westward, must learn to work together, to fuse our interests, and to become as one. This we must do if we were to survive and become a town.

No settlement lay nearer than Fort Bridger, more than a hundred miles to the southwest . . . or so we had heard.

All about us was Indian country, and we were few.

There were seven men to do the building, two boys to guard our stock, and thirteen women and children to gather wood and buffalo chips for the fires of the nights to come, and kindling against a time of snow.

Only now did we realize that we were strangers, and each looked upon the other with distant eyes, judging and being judged, uneasy and causing uneasiness, for here we had elected to make our stand, and we knew not the temper of those with whom we stood.

It was Ruth Macken, but lately become a widow, who led the move to stop while supplies remained to us, and we who stood beside her were those who favored her decision and joined with her in stopping.

My father had been a Bible-reading man and named his sons from the Book. Four of our brothers had gone the way of flesh, and of the boys only we two remained. Cain, a wedded man with two children, and I, Bendigo Shafter, eighteen and a man with hands to work.

Our sister was with us. Lorna was a pretty sixteen, named for a cousin in Wales.

"You will build for the Widow Macken," Cain said to me. "Her Bud is a man for his twelve years, but young for the lifting of logs and the notching."

So I went up the hill through the frost of the morning, pausing when I reached the bench where their cabin would stand. A fair place it was, with a cold spring spilling its water down to the meadow where our oxen and horses grazed upon the brown grass of autumn. Tall pines, sentinel straight, made a park of the bench, and upon the steep slope behind there was a good stand of timber.

The view from the bench was a fine one, and I stood to look upon it, filling myself with the quiet morning and the beauty of the long valley below the Beaver Rim.

"You have an eye for beauty, Mr. Shafter," Ruth Macken said to me, and I kept my eyes from her, feeling the flush and the heat climbing my neck as it forever did when a pretty woman spoke to me. "It is a good thing in a man."

"It works a magic," I said, "to look upon distance."

"Some people can't abide it. Bigness makes them feel small instead of offering a challenge, but I am glad my Bud will grow to manhood here. A big country can breed big men."

"Yes, ma'am." I glanced about the bench. "I have come to build you a cabin, then."

"Build it so when spring comes I can add a long room on the south, for when the wagons roll again I shall open a trading post."

She turned to Bud, who had come up the slope from the meadow. "You will help Mr. Shafter and learn from him. It is not every man who can build a house."

Ruth Macken had a way of making a man feel large in his tracks, so what could I do but better than my best?

The morning chill spoke of winter coming, yet I notched each log with care and trimmed them with smooth, even blows.

There is a knowledge in the muscles of a workman that goes beyond the mind, a skill that lies in the flesh and the fiber, and my hands and heart held a love for the wood, the good wood whose fresh chips fell cleanly to the left and the right.

Yet as I worked my thoughts worried over the problem of our town. We were ill-prepared for winter, although our sudden decision to stop left us better off than had we pushed on to the westward.

Going on would have been simple, for travel is an escape, and as long as our wagons moved our decisions could be postponed. When one moves, one is locked in the treadmill of travel, and all decisions must await a destination. By choosing to stop we had brought our refuge tumbling about us, and our problems could no longer be avoided.

The promised land is always a distant land, aglow with golden fire. It is a land one never attains, for once attained one faces fulfillment and the knowledge that whatever a land may promise, it may also demand a payment of courage and strength.

To destroy is easy, to build is hard. To scoff is also easy, but to go on in the face of scoffing and to do what is right is the way of a man.

Neely Stuart already regretted the stopping and spoke of continuing on to California in the spring, and Tom Croft, who listened to Neely, was a man who never knew whether the course he had taken was the right one. So he was always open to persuasion. Nor was his Mary of a different mind.

Even Webb talked of going on when spring should again bring grass to the hills, yet he had been the first to break off from the wagon train and follow Ruth Macken in her decision. He was a discontented, irritable man, always impatient for change, yet he was also strong and resolute and would stand up in an emergency. He had a son, an arrogant, disagreeable boy named Foss . . . short for Foster.

John Sampson, my brother Cain, and I were for staying on, which left only Ethan Sackett, a single man who had been guide for the wagon train but had chosen to leave it when we did.

"What has he to do with us?" Webb demanded, when I wondered aloud if Sackett would stay on. "He's a drifter, not one of us."

"He chose to stay with us, and that makes him one of us."

"He chose to stay because of Mrs. Macken. Would he have come with us had it not been for her? I say he does not belong here."

It was our first night around the fire, the first after leaving the wagon train, and we huddled close to the flames for there was an autumn chill in the night. The truth was we were all a little frightened at what we had done, and our nerves were on edge because of it.

"He won't be with us long," Neely Stuart said. "His kind have no stability. He is more like an Indian than a white man."

"Who among us," John Sampson said mildly, "has wintered in this country? I think before the winter is gone we shall be glad he is among us."

"We could have been miles from here," Stuart complained. "We were fools to stop."

"Mrs. Macken," I told them, "will open a store, come spring."

"To sell what?" Stuart scoffed. "And to whom?"

"She will sell boots and clothing she and her husband packed against that purpose and vegetables we ourselves will raise. Whenever possible she will accept goods in payment, goods to be sold again."

"A silly woman's dream!"

"There might be good trade with the wagon trains," Webb admitted, "but no matter. When it is warm again I shall move on."

"I shall stay."

It was the calm voice of my brother, to whom all men listened. Until then he had remained silent, watching the leap of the flames and thinking his thoughts.

Cain's face was square, massive, and might have been hewn from oak. His body was also square, but large and powerful. He moved easily, as one who is in complete command of himself and his every muscle. He was not a man given to talking, speaking only when his mind was made up, not as many men do who shape their thoughts as they speak.

"I shall open my smithy and a shop for the mending of guns. I believe the Widow Macken knows what she is about."

"Stay on if you wish," Stuart said defensively.

"I shall not." Yet his tone had weakened before the weight of my brother's decision.

"I shall leave with the first grass," Tom Croft said. "The wilderness and the thought of Indians distresses my wife."

The sickness of disappointment lay upon me, for if they left our strength would be pared to nothing, and we must also go. We were too few as it was, and if attacked by Indians our chances would be slight.

This valley we had chosen lay upon a highroad for the Shoshone, but it was traveled by the Sioux as well and occasionally by the Ute or Blackfeet. Our presence invited trouble.

On the morning I went up the slope to build for the Widow Macken. There was a fringe of ice along the stream's edge, and the meadow was white with frost. My breath showed in a cloud, and the bodies of the cattle steamed as they worked, hauling down the logs after I felled the trees. . . .

When I had felled my third tree, I put Bud to trimming the limbs, watching him first to be sure he knew the use of an axe, for this was no country in which to be left without a foot. I was beginning the fourth tree when Ethan Sackett rode up the hill to draw rein beside me.

He leaned on the pommel of his saddle and watched for a moment before he spoke. "Bendigo, at this time of year there will be few Indians about, but do you take a walk up the ridge now and again to look over the country. If they are about we must know it, so keep your eyes wide for a sign."

"You believe they are holed up for the winter?"

"Soon . . . but a body can't be too caring. Bendigo, I count on you. I cut little ice with those men down yonder, but neither do I pay it much mind. But if there's trouble comes I figure you'll stand. You and that brother of yours."

"Webb will fight. I have a feeling you can count on him, too. He's a mean, cantankerous man, but come fightin' time, he'll be around."

"You are right, I am thinking. You keep shy of that man, Bendigo. He's dangerous...."

Of a sudden there was a pounding of hoofs, and Ethan turned sharply around, his gun half-drawn under his buckskin shirt.

It was Neely Stuart. He leaned from his horse, trying to peer into the door. "Is Mae here? She went out with the little Shafter girl and Lenny Sampson."

"They were over in the creek bottom when I was cuttin' poles atop the ridge. They should be back by now."

A gust whipped snow into our faces and there was a moan in the wind. For a moment the wind caught our breath and we could not speak.

"Come on!" Neely said. "We'll roust out ever'-body and hunt for them."

You go out there with a lot of tenderfeet," Ethan said, "and you'll lose some of them."

"Who asked you?" Neely shouted. "That's my sister out there!"

Ethan was in no way put out by Neely's anger. "How much experience have you had in blizzards, Stuart? A man can lose himself in fifty yards, and judging by the sound of the wind, this one will be pretty bad."

"Ethan's right," I admitted. "You can't even see the other houses now."

"You coming or not?"

"We're coming," Ethan said. He turned to Ruth Macken. "You'll be all right, ma'am?"

"Bud's here, and we've some unpacking to do and a meal to get. When you come back, come to supper. I'll have some hot soup waiting."

We rode down to town, unable to talk for the wind blowing our words down our throats, yet we thought of what was to come; not one of us was fixed for winter.

It was amazing the way the snow piled up. In the

few minutes it had been falling there were two to three inches on the level, and it was starting to drift against the north side of the cabins.

Neely had reached Cain's house ahead of us, and when we came through the door accompanied by a gust of blown snow he was talking. ". . . if that Sackett opens his mouth in here, I'll . . . !"

"Whatever it is you'll do," Ethan said mildly, "you'd better save it until later. We've got to find those youngsters before they freeze to death."

"You stay out of this!" Stuart shouted. He turned on the others. "Scatter out and hunt for them!"

Ethan squatted on his heels against the wall. "You'd be wanderin' blind in the snow. You start seven men out in a storm like this and some of them aren't comin' back. You've got women-folks will need you before spring comes."

Neely started to shout, but Cain stopped him with a gesture. "What did you have in mind?"

"Bendigo here, he saw those young uns down along the creek, and if they were doin' what I figure, they never saw that storm comin'."

He turned his eyes to Cain Shafter. "I should do the hunting because I know this country better than anybody here, and there ain't anybody going to mind if I don't come back. I'd like Bendigo, if he'd care to come along."

"What about me?" Webb demanded. "I grew up in snow country. I seen a sight of it."

"You're welcome. I spoke of Bendigo because he's single and he's steady. Doesn't fly off the handle. A blizzard in this country is nothing to play around with."

"While you sit here talking those youngsters are freezing!" Neely's voice shook with anger. "Don't you try to tell me what to do! I'm going out!"

"All right. Where do you figure to look?"

"Out there!" Neely flung a wide arm.

"Big country." Ethan got to his feet. "Better take it slow. You get warmed up and you start to sweat. The first time you slow down or stop to rest the sweat will freeze, and you'll be wearing a thin coat of ice next your skin."

"You think they stayed with the creek?" Cain asked.

"Sure. There's hawthorn along the creek, and my guess is they found some late berries hanging. Sometimes they stay on until January, and the first day here I rode down there and saw the bushes heavy with them. Those young uns are hungry for sweet, and it's there, so they probably just went on from bush to bush. When they realized it was snowing heavy they probably stayed right there, knowing we'd come for them."

Ordinarily that would be good thinking, but knowing how flighty Mae Stuart was, I couldn't see her using that much judgment. Mae was sixteen and pretty, but mighty notional. She'd put up her hair about a year back, and she was flouncy, feeling her oats, like. She'd been making eyes at men-folks since she was shy of thirteen and was getting to where she wanted to do something about it.

Ann Shafter, Cain's oldest, was only ten. Lenny Sampson, although a bright youngster, was six . . .

The cold was intense. Here or there the snow had heaped itself over a fallen tree or some rocks to form a hollow where an animal or child might have curled up, so we dared pass none of them. Once, slipping on an icy log hidden beneath the snow, I had a bad fall.

When I got up I saw Ethan squatted on his heels, studying something.

It was a rabbit snare, rigged at the opening of a run. The snow around the snare was disturbed and there were flecks of blood, most of them partly covered by snow. Ethan put a finger on the thickest spot of blood, and it smeared slightly under pressure. Almost frozen, but not quite.

"Indians," he said.

We felt a chill beyond that of the cold. Within the hour, no doubt much less than that, an Indian had taken a rabbit from that snare and killed it. He must have been inspecting his snares at the same time that the children were along the creek.

Webb was a hard man, but he had a child of his own, and he knew these children. "Injuns!" he said. "Injuns got them."

The tracks that might have told us more lay under the new fallen snow, and the storm was growing worse. It was only by chance that we had found the snare, for in a few minutes it would have been covered.

We had thought to find the children before they could freeze, perhaps huddled somewhere out of the wind waiting for us . . .

There was nothing to do but go back home. There was a chance they had found their way back, but nobody would have bet on it.

Ethan fell in beside me as we started back. He had faced directly away from that clump of trees, taken the wind at a certain angle on his face, and led off. It was the only guide in a storm like that, and although the wind might shift it wasn't likely to shift that much at this stage of the storm.

"Bendigo, are you game to take a chance? I've a notion where those Indians might be."

"Just the two of us?"

"We'd not make it out and back tonight. Are you with me?"

To my dying day I shall remember that blizzard. Ethan moved up to Cain, who had taken over breaking trail. "Hold across the wind," he advised. "Let it take you on the left eye and nose, like. You'll reach sight of the valley in a few minutes. Once over that low ridge, hold along the edge of the trees above Mrs. Macken's and you'll make it."

Cain stopped. He turned his broad back square to

the wind and looked at Ethan. "What about you?"

"Bendigo an' me, we've an idea. If worst comes to worst we'll just dig a hole in the snow and sit it out. A man can wait out a storm if he doesn't exhaust himself first."

We faced into the storm and plodded away, leaning against the wind. Darkness had come upon us, and the wind blew a full gale, cutting at our exposed brows like knives. It seemed an age before we climbed a knoll and stumbled into a thick stand of aspen where we stopped to catch our breath.

"The day we fetched up to this place," Ethan explained, "I spotted the sign of eight to ten Indians with their travois, lodges, and goods. Not wanting to frighten the women-folks I said nothing. Maybe they were passing through, but that snare was reset, so I figure they're close by."

It was almost still inside the aspen grove. The slim trunks stood so close they formed a barrier against the wind.

"The best place for those Indians to wait out a storm is in the hollow right below this hill, so we're a-goin' down there."

Cold or not, I loosened the buttons on my coat and laid a hand to that old pistol of mine. Never in my born days had I drawn against any man, and I had no mind to unless the need was great.

"You keep that handy. An Indian respects strength but mighty little else."

We went down the hill through the deepening snow, smelling smoke on the wind, and sure enough, the lodges were there, three of them, covered with snow except around the smoke hole at the top where the warmth had melted the snow away.

We listened outside each lodge until we heard Mae speak and some arguing among the Indians. Ethan lifted the flap and went in, with me right behind him.

A small fire burned in the center of the tent, and the air was stifling hot and smoky after the cold outside. Right off I spotted Mae and the youngsters beside her. They seemed unhurt, only scared.

There were five buck Indians in there. One young brave was on his feet arguing, and he was mad as all get-out.

The others were older, and the one at whom the buck seemed to be pointing his words was oldest of all. Now that one might be old, but his eyes were clear, and it seemed to me I saw a gleam of malice in those eyes, like maybe he didn't like that young buck too much.

Talk broke off when we came in, and the young brave put a hand to his tomahawk. The next thing I knew he was looking into the business end of my six-shooter.

Now he was no more surprised than I, for I'd no thought of drawing that gun. It just fetched out when the need came, and young as that warrior was, he knew what that gun meant, and he let go of his tomahawk like it was red hot.

Ethan Sackett, he started talking to that old Indian in Shoshone.

After a minute he stopped talking, and the old man spoke. Ethan interpreted for me out of the side of his mouth. "The young buck wants to keep Mae and kill the young uns, but the old man doesn't like it. He says the Shoshone are friends to the white man.

"He's right about that, but there's more to this argument than a body can see at first glimpse. I think the old man wants to take that young buck down a peg. Gettin' too big for his britches."

My eyes had never left that young warrior. He was mad as a trapped catamount and ready to pitch in and go to fighting.

"Tell them we are friends, Ethan, and tell them to come when the snow leaves and trade with us. Tell them to bring their furs, hides, or whatever.

And thank them for saving the young ones from the snow. Tell them when they come in the spring we will have presents for them."

Sackett, he talked for a while, but before the old man could reply that young buck busted in with a furious harangue, gestering now and again toward the other lodges, like he was about to go for help.

"We'd best take the youngsters and light out," I suggested. "This shapes up to trouble."

Ethan never turned his head. "Mae, get up and come over here and bring the young uns with you."

When the young buck saw what was happening he started to yell, and I belted him in the stomach with my fist. When he doubled over I sledged him across the skull with my gun barrel.

Not one of the others so much as moved, but the old man said something I didn't catch. They didn't seem much upset by what had happened.

Ethan took out his tobacco sack and passed it to the old man, with a gesture implying it was to be shared with the others. Me, I took out my Shafter-made axe, the best there is, and handed it to the old man.

"Friend," I said. Then indicating the axe I said, "It is a medicine axe, made from iron from the skies."

"The youngsters first," Ethan said, "then you."

"I'm holding the gun. You go ahead of me."

We floundered through the snow, which was growing deeper by the moment, and made slow time until we got to the crest of the ridge. My heart was pumping heavily when we topped out, and far off, behind us, we heard shouts.

Ethan led the way, but not toward home. With the youngsters to see to we were in no shape to tackle a trip home through the night and the storm. So Ethan took us into a hollow downwind of the Indians. It was a place gouged out by the fall of two pines whose roots had torn up great masses of earth that clung to a frozen spider web of roots.

When Ethan waded into the hollow he was shoulder-deep, but he floundered around, tramping down the snow. When I saw what he was about, I helped. We tramped down an area five or six feet across, but with snow walls five feet high facing the triangle made by the roots, it was all of eight feet high.

Scooping out a hollow big enough for the kids in one snow wall, I packed the snow tight with my hands.

Ethan found some heavy, broken limbs with which he made a platform for our fire, then he dug under the fallen trees for broken twigs and bark. Soon we had a small fire going, using the mass of earth and roots for a reflector.

We broke off evergreen branches and made a roof across the corner of our hole, and with the falling snow to cover it we soon had a snug snow-house.

We were much too close to the Shoshone camp, and it was a worrisome thing to be without rifles. We had six-shooters, and each of us carried a spare loaded cylinder to be slipped into place if we emptied our guns.

Ann fell asleep in my arms, and Mae put her head on my shoulder, snuggling closer, I thought, than need be. Ethan fixed a bough bed for Lenny Sampson, and he was off to sleep, a mighty tired little boy.

Ethan looked across the fire at me. "We got us a family, Bendigo. Likely the only one I'll ever have."

"You've got no kin?"

He added sticks to the fire. "I've kin-folk a-plenty although I don't recall seeing any of them for years. One was a mountain man like me, a Sackett from the Cumberland River country of Tennessee. Ran into him at a rendezvous on the Green.

"I don't lack for kin-folk. There's Sacketts all over Tennessee and Carolina, but I lack somebody of my very own. When I was shy of fourteen my pa was killed by Comanches on the Sante Fe Trail. Since then I've fetched up and down the country from Missouri to the shores of the western sea, but I hunger for a place of my own and somebody to do for."

Cain's daughter Ann had gone right off to sleep like Lenny, but that Mae was making me nervous, acting like she was asleep but snuggling like she was about to crawl into my lap. If Ethan noticed he paid it no mind.

Bendigo works hard to help his family, friends and neighbors build the settlement. He has many fast-action adventures in this treacherous wilderness before setting off for the East and a career as a newspaperman.

Read the complete Bantam Book, available September 1st, wherever paperbacks are sold.

BANTAM'S #1
ALL-TIME BESTSELLING AUTHOR
AMERICA'S FAVORITE WESTERN WRITER

☐	12879	THE KEY-LOCK MAN	$1.75
☐	12925	RADIGAN	$1.75
☐	12631	WAR PARTY	$1.75
☐	12986	KIOWA TRAIL	$1.75
☐	12732	THE BURNING HILLS	$1.75
☐	12064	SHALAKO	$1.75
☐	12670	KILRONE	$1.75
☐	11119	THE RIDER OF LOST CREEK	$1.50
☐	12424	CALLAGHEN	$1.75
☐	12063	THE QUICK AND THE DEAD	$1.75
☐	12729	OVER ON THE DRY SIDE	$1.75
☐	13057	DOWN THE LONG HILLS	$1.75
☐	12721	TO THE FAR BLUE MOUNTAINS	$1.75
☐	10491	WESTWARD THE TIDE	$1.50
☐	12043	KID RODELO	$1.75
☐	12887	BROKEN GUN	$1.75
☐	13151	WHERE THE LONG GRASS BLOWS	$1.75
☐	12519	HOW THE WEST WAS WON	$1.75

Buy them at your local bookstore or use this handy coupon for ordering: